Pacific Pack

Book 1: Coastal Wolves

Printed in the United States of America: First Printing, 2023.

ISBN 978-1-959981-05-3 (eBook)
ISBN 978-1-959981-04-6 (paperback)

http://www.hannahwillow217.wordpress.com

Copy/Line Editor: Angela Grimes
Editor: Weslee Imrisek
Cover Art: Getcovers.com
Formatting: Huckleberry Rahr

Coastal Wolves:
1: Pacific Pack
2: Wolf Magic
3: Campus Prowl
4: Loan Wolf
5: Pack Triage
6: Mystical Science
7: Lupine Investigation

Dedication:

I want to thank all the people who encourage me every day. Angela Grimes brings light and goofy, a bit of daily joy. Weslee Imrisek is forever encouraging me. They are my sunshine. My family has more confidence in me than any author could ever ask for. Elizabeth Daly will read all my books, regardless of if they are her preferred genre. If that doesn't give a person confidence, I don't know what will. And Nicole Maness, who after reading this book wanted to know when she could read the rest ... well, my friend, I'm working on it!

Chapter 1 - Running with ... Coyotes

The wind tickled her face, the leaves and branches scraped her muzzle, the scents of the woods filled her snout—she ran. Feeling the pull of the moon, running through the woods, and hunting ... Tamsin loved everything about being a werewolf. The scents—the woods, the wet soil, the animals around her—called to her senses. A deep breath brought her a distant whiff of a doe, but a lone wolf couldn't bring down a deer and give her the honorable death she deserved.

Moonlight illuminated the small, open field she cut across. Tamsin slowed. Being alone, she needed to be wary of other predators.

The series of sharp yips sounded from her left. She stopped and lowered herself into the long grass. Tamsin lifted her nose and sniffed. Coyotes, two or three. Taking a deeper breath, she separated what she could smell. Three, definitely three of the beasts.

"When fighting alone, don't let the opposition get behind you, dear."

"But, Dad, if I'm out there alone, how do I control what the other people do?"

He reached out and ruffled my hair, the auburn waves passing back and forth in front of my eyes. "That's why we have the pack, Tam. You're never alone when you have your family."

Tamsin shook herself from the memory. She'd been alone since her dad died over five years earlier, and in that time, she'd learned to fight without a pack.

With one more pull of the air, she tried to figure out where the three opponents were. She inched backwards before she realized one of the beasts had circled around her while she'd given over to reminiscence.

She slunk to the right until she could see the small reddish-brown animal. One-on-one, she knew she could take it down. As a wolf, she was larger than average, much bigger than the coyotes. A quick scan told her the other two were far enough away. It was worth the risk.

She pounced, her jaw coming down on the animal's neck. Bones cracked with a quick jerk of her maw. The weight of the animal's carcass dragged her head down. She dropped the dead enemy. *One down, two to go.*

Before she could get the coyote's fur from her teeth, pain radiated up from her back leg. Tamsin whipped around and saw a small beast, brown and raggedy, locked onto her hind leg. She growled low to avoid alerting the local pack of her whereabouts. They were running just north of her, and it wasn't safe to let more predators know she was wounded.

She reared up and spun, landing with her front paws in the newcomer's belly. The move just caused the coyote to dig his teeth in deeper.

The third coyote darted out of the brush, low and fast, aiming for Tamsin's belly. Tamsin rolled, barely avoiding his teeth and evisceration.

She snapped as the attacker passed over her and

got a piece of the third coyote's haunch. Blood splashed her face as the coyote barked loud enough to wake the dead.

Suddenly, Tamsin was free from both coyotes' teeth, but they had her in their sights. She knew they'd be on her if she ran. Testing her leg, she couldn't put too much weight on it. As the coyotes flanked her, ready to pounce, she knew she couldn't make the first move. She had to wait for their attack to react.

Tamsin watched them, her head jerking back and forth, waiting, wondering if this was her time. Even if she won, she wasn't sure she could make it back to her car if she sustained one more injuries. Should she have accepted the invitation to the Chicago Pack? No, that would've never worked. She couldn't be a pack member under just any alpha; her dominance level was too high. Being a lone wolf had made more sense ... until she ended up alone in a fight for her life.

A streak of dark gray flew from the tree line, slamming into the larger of the two coyotes, knocking it aside, she knew she'd gotten it out of the picture for a moment. Immediately, Tamsin pounced on the other one, her jaw coming down hard on the animal's neck, tearing deeply to end the fight fast.

With a quick glance at the other attacker—a werewolf—she realized it was her client, Nolan

Barn. Before Nolan could size her up, Tamsin fled. Her gait was more of a limping walk than a run, but she didn't think the other werewolf would follow. Tamsin wasn't part of the pack, and protocol dictated Nolan check in with his alpha first. To be safe, Tamsin made her way to a stream and limped through it for a mile before climbing out and heading towards her car. It was bad enough she would hear about Nolan's aid the next time they worked out together; she didn't also need his comments about how dominant a werewolf she was.

As Tamsin ended her run, her stomach cramped. *I'm going to need food before I'm going to be able to shift and heal my injuries. I've pushed myself hard tonight.* Slowing down, she searched and found the scent of a rabbit. She took in a long pull of air and smelled no other wolves nearby. Without making a sound, she slunk in low and quiet. She approached the fat bunny, mouth watering at the idea of meat. At the last moment, before it could run, she scooped the rabbit up in her teeth and gave a sharp shake, breaking its neck.

The animal only satiated a bit of Tamsin's hunger, so she ran as best she could on her three good legs, hunting again. As she searched, she moved slowly towards civilization. It was late, and though she loved running as a wolf, the human needed to be up early, bright-eyed and bushy-tailed, to teach high school English the next day. No more gallivanting and playing.

She found a pair of voles. Not her favorite, but they'd give her the energy she needed to shift, and she could eat more when she got home. Afterwards, her belly felt full; all she wanted to do was take a nap, but she forced herself onward until she found her car.

Light drops of rain began to fall, splashing bits of dirt and dust into her eyes. With a grumble, she began to shift back. It hurt more than normal with her bleeding leg, but after a few minutes she lay on her back in human form, panting. She checked the damage. No broken bones, just a few deep gashes. Opening her trunk, she found her first-aid kit and applied antibiotic cream and a bandage. Good enough.

She grabbed her clothes and slipped them on. Although being nude didn't bother her, the humans didn't like naked people running around their city, even inside a car. It was time to head towards Chicago and her apartment for some much-needed sleep. As scary as the wolves and coyotes were, high school students could smell any weakness, and they *would* eat her alive.

CHAPTER 2 - WORK WILL KILL YOU

Paige wore her swimsuit with a tank top and sweatshirt to keep warm from the cool breeze coming from the ocean. Three families sat on the beach watching the steel blue water that matched the dark sky. None of the tourists that had come frost the Santa Cruz Boardwalk seemed to have made it down to the beach today. The water was just too cold. Everyone here was a regular; she recognized their setups.

She debated closing her umbrella and letting the

sun warm her. Checking out the other two lifeguards on duty, they appeared to be as bored as she was. The chance anyone would go more than ankle deep into the water was very low. She didn't think her day could get any worse; working a slow day at the beach was as tedious and boring as watching paint dry.

Her mind wandered to the book she was writing. *I wonder if I could add something about the beach or a creature from the ocean to my book? The kraken came from below, terrorizing the crew of the ship as his mighty tentacles—*

Her phone rang, pulling her from her plotting. The display read *Boss Man - D.* "Hey, Dominik."

"Paige, got a lead on a story. Downtown. Need you there now." His voice was brisk and distracted. Paige could hear voices and typing in the background. The online paper's office was always a hive of activity. She wished she could work there full-time, but the money wasn't enough.

"I'm at the beach."

"It's a murder, Paige. You're our best writer for these stories."

One more look at the three families and Paige made up her mind. Waving her rescue tube, she got the other two guards' attention. She signaled she was leaving. They nodded their agreement. Three guards weren't needed on such a slow day. "Okay, send me the address; I'm on my way."

She signed off with Dominik and headed to the locker room where she changed into jeans and a t-shirt. In her supervisor's office, she told him she was heading out. With an empty beach Paige was unsurprised that the supervisor was fine with paying one less lifeguard for the day.

Paige jogged a few blocks to find her ten-year-old Honda Civic and headed to the address Dominik texted to her. She had to park a block away because of all the emergency vehicles in the area. A murder was big business.

Once she got to the scene, she saw the body being covered, medical personnel focused on it, cops putting down numbered yellow plastic tents and taking pictures, other officials holding people back, and many onlookers watching everything. Phones were out everywhere as spectators tried to get their own images of the gruesome scene.

Off to one side stood Officer Rey Summers, a friend and contact she used for her stories to ensure her articles were accurate. Officer Summers looked busy, but Paige could get some preliminary notes down while she waited. She figured this would be where she spent the rest of her day.

There was a lot of blood. She had gotten a momentary glimpse of the man before the sheet covered him. His neck and gut looked eaten by something wild.

Paige began writing questions in her notepad:

Could wild animals have come into the center of town and attacked some random person? Which animal wondered this far from the wilderness? Did the human capture the animal, bring it here, and lose control? Was the animal wild or domestic before it attacked the person? If the animal was a pet, why attack the human? Is the person local or a tourist?

She started a new page. *If not an animal kill, did it start as a mugging gone wrong? How did the person end up here? Where did he come from?*

She snapped a few pictures. The body on the ground, the blood on the wall, and the number of areas from which the police collected evidence. As she worked, the officers tried to disperse the crowd. She saw that Officer Summers had moved to crowd control. When he got close enough, she waved. "Will you have time to talk today?"

"Later," the man sighed. "This is big, Paige. It happened midday during tourist season. I'll tell you right now that he was a tourist, the death was brutal, and there were no witnesses. He has his wallet and keys and all his money, so it wasn't a mugging gone wrong. Beyond that, it'll take some time. I've gotta go."

Paige found a bench under a lamp across the street and fleshed out her notes. She took a few more photos and began doing some research. *Who were the tourist groups in town? What animals were most likely to attack the neck and gut?* Anything that could help her story once Officer Summers could give her more.

Time passed slowly, and she realized the sun had gone down. Her stomach grumbled and she debated getting a burger and fries. Some of her notes were written, some were voice notes on things she wanted to research later. Looking up, the alley was cleared of everything and everyone. She sent a quick text to Officer Summers, and the officer said he'd email Paige tomorrow.

With a sigh, Paige debated what to do next. She had a bunch of notes and a good idea of what had happened. She needed to get more information. She decided to organize her notes first while everything was clear in her mind and the alley was in front of her, then dinner, then home for sleep.

Bending over her notes, she lost herself to the organization of her thoughts. She needed to figure out where the tourist came from. There were so many questions about the animal, she debated starting to look some stuff up on her phone. She tapped the possible research tool in her pocket, but figured the battery was dead. She started a list of priorities for the next few days.

A sledgehammer slammed into her side. She landed on the ground with a stab of piercing pain radiating throughout her body. *God above, what was that?* She jerked her head down to see a beast with glowing eyes gnawing on her side. Agony erupted everywhere. Arms trembling, she swung, but the contact did nothing to dislodge the monster. It kept ... oh, God ... it kept eating her. She kicked and tried to get away, but nothing helped.

"Help!" She wasn't sure if she yelled it or only thought it. *I'm being eaten alive!*

CHAPTER 3 - A DAY IN THE LIFE ...

"A werewolf who's also a vegetarian!"
"No! A vampire who's a vegetarian and can't stand the smell of blood."
"Oh, maybe the two together. A romance."
Tamsin sighed. "No romances. I'm not reading any of that from any of you. Creativity is great—your ideas are wonderful—but you're all too young for the naughty scenes ... and if you're not, then I'm too old to read it."

The students in her Creative Writing class laughed. They were seniors and only a few months from graduating. The class was an elective and only students who wanted to be there were.

"What about aliens from different planets who each engineer a different gene. They can't procreate so they have to work together for the advancement of each world's survival, but the worlds have been at war for generations?"

Tamsin smiled as her students threw out more and more ideas, each one more elaborate than the last. She wrote their ideas on the whiteboard at the front of the room, hoping to ignite the creative excitement in the quieter students who weren't participating.

As much as she enjoyed the class, it was the last period on Friday, and the day couldn't end soon enough. The bell rang at half past three, and the students filed out. One student stayed back, deciding it was her job to erase the board. Tamsin didn't mind since she didn't love doing the task herself.

"Ms. Hath, wouldn't it be amazing if there really were werewolves or vampires?" She erased a section of the board. "Or witches! Just think of it."

She watched the student's blond ponytail sway as she erased more of the words she'd spent the last fifty minutes writing. "Are you hoping for a sparkly vampire to woo you as you choose between him and some honorable werewolf, Megan? Two young men to watch you play soccer, then fight over you after your team wins?"

A blush climbed up her face. "No! And that isn't the only series I read. And sparkling vampires are ridiculous. I think I'd rather be a witch than something that craves blood. Both of those creatures ... " She shivered. "Anyway, I think I'll enjoy writing about them and be glad it's all make believe."

Grabbing her bag, she skipped from the room.

Tamsin watched her and sighed. Make believe. *I wonder how long the existence of werewolves and witches will remain hidden. Cell phones, hidden cameras, and the free-flowing information of the internet makes it harder and harder to hide. Once it is out and believed, life will get much more difficult for all of us.*

She packed up her bag of work to do at home over the weekend, and left the building. She got into her Subaru Solterra, and headed to the gym. The only way she could make ends meet was to have two jobs. She had a training session with Nolan and would find out if the pack werewolf had recognized her the other night during her run.

Nolan had already arrived. A few inches taller, with short red hair and blue eyes, the wiry man sat on an exercise bike warming up.

Though the gym was packed—*didn't people have jobs? It's just after four in the afternoon on a Friday!* —the bike next to Nolan was available. Tamsin adjusted the seat and began her own warm-up.

After a few minutes Nolan spoke, his voice breathy as he pushed himself. "I'm glad you could meet with me a third time this week. I know that ... um ... *this* ... week is hard."

He meant the week of the full moon. Tamsin usually only met with Nolan once on a week this busy, but she needed the money. She recently got the fully electric car, and as much as she loved it, a new car was expensive.

"What can I say; you've worn me down. We're both obviously out of shape and need much more gym time. Now, this is a warm-up, not a sprint. Slow down."

Nolan jerked, and she realized she'd used a bit of her power. Shutting her eyes, she worked on building up her walls. She couldn't remember the last time she'd been so sloppy; maybe when she was a teen. Gods above! She needed to do something to get her head on straight. Maybe she'd call her aunt tonight. That would help her get grounded. Her aunt was the last of her living family and she needed that connection, even if it were only over the phone.

"Sorry Nolan, I just meant ... let's move onto something else."

Eyes a bit wild, Nolan gaped at her. "What the

hell did you just do? On Wednesday, I felt something too when I helped you with your ... issue. How are you, by the way? You're walking better now than you were then. After checking in with the big honcho, I tried to find you, but you'd disappeared. Now, tell me what you're hiding! Am I imagining things? Is this why you refuse to join our pack?"

Tamsin's shoulders drooped. "Can we just move on? Forget the last minute just happened? You're mistaken about the severity of my wound; I was fine. As for ... joining your group, if I joined you all in Chicago, I would upset my old Santa Cruz crew. They are tender souls." I didn't think anyone listened to us or would think 'pack' meant anything, but one couldn't be too careful.

"You know that isn't true. Your pack knows you live here now," Nolan spoke softly, knowing werewolves had good hearing. They were at the weights, and no one was close to them. Tamsin led him with signals. Nolan continued his pitch. "Didn't your uncle pass away recently? So, the alpha isn't even related to you anymore. You should really think about joining us. You could be an asset. You know ..." he looked around at the full gym and seemed to decide a soft voice wasn't enough, "...our type, we need people, touch, connection. Being a lone ... er, alone, isn't healthy for you. How long has it been?"

Tamsin shook her head. "Nolan, I'm fine. I've heard your arguments before, but I don't think it would be a good idea. This is better, trust me. I get some connection working with you and teaching. Believe me, I know what I'm doing."

The other werewolf shook his head. "I don't think you do, friend. Remember, we're here for you."

A couple hours later, Tamsin sat in her living room, freshly showered and fed. She'd made chili for dinner. She'd learned that cooking was a great way to meditate and calm herself.

"Mom, why are you cross-stitching that picture of a dragon?" I watched in amazement as the picture came to life.

"We all need to find an activity that helps clear our mind from the day, Tam, this is mine, and I love creating art that other people can enjoy."

"Who is that for?" I bit my lip, waiting for her answer.

Tamsin hugged the pillow her mom made her with the dragon art embroidery sewn to the top to her chest. Tired, she debated not calling her aunt, but knew it was the right decision. Dialing her number, her voice was another balm on her soul.

"Tamsin! I'm glad you called. How are things in the windy city?"

"I'm good. How are you holding up, Aunt Elinore?"

There was a pause, and her voice dropped. "You know, I'm allowed to be okay. You don't have to always remind me that Clyde died. I still have my coven. You remember Cinthia; you met her a few times before you left. I don't know if you know many of the others. We have some fresh meat in the circle."

She laughed. "Training up a new bunch of hellions to take over the world?"

"You know it! Now, when are you returning? The new alphas are awful. They're terrorizing the city. A person was attacked the other day, and I swear it was the pack out of control, probably Steve. I swear that man is nuttier than a five-pound fruit cake. Your dad and uncle would've never allowed that."

She stilled, thinking about her words. "You think they killed someone, and that Steve is out of control? Is there a reason he would attack this person?"

"All I know is there was something over the police call: person attacked by wild animal downtown. They were taken to the morgue. It's all hush-hush for now. I'm waiting for The Daily Cruz story to come out about it."

Tamsin rubbed her forehead. She felt a headache coming on. "Well, if Vernon and Steve are getting that bold, you need to stay watchful. Let your coven know as well. Let's set up a weekly call. I really don't like this. I know you and the other witches are strong, but werewolves are sneaky and dangerous."

"I love you too, Tamsin. I'd feel better if you were close. Want to move back home?"

"Spring break is in a couple of weeks, and then summer break comes a bit after that. Maybe I'll drive out and spend the summer with you. I'd feel better if you had more backup."

"Thinking of moving back then?" She persisted.

"No, Aunt Elinore. I like my life in Chicago. You know I don't want to fight for control of the pack out there, and I won't be part of it as anything less than alpha. Love you. Talk to you soon." Hanging up, she lay back and contemplated the reasons Vernon, the Santa Cruz alpha, had for harming a random human. His actions were coming too close to outing the werewolves.

CHAPTER 4 - IS THIS HEAVEN OR HELL?

Paige woke up in a room she didn't recognize. The bed was softer than hers. The wall was a dark purple and off-white stripe. It must be day time because light streamed in from the window above the bed, and her body felt stiff lying on its side.

With a groan, she stretched and rolled to her back.

"You're finally awake, young one."

She let her head fall to the side and saw two men sitting in wooden chairs on the other side of the room. One was a thick shorter man with black wavy hair and brown eyes. He had an air of ... something—Paige wasn't sure what—about him. He looked like the type who took out his anger with fists.

The other had a soft smile, taller, with short blond hair and blue eyes. He could be any surfer Paige saw hitting the waves on the beach. She wondered if she had seen him before.

She wondered if they had a dog and had just washed it, they smelled ... furry. She rubbed her nose.

Narrowing her eyes at them, she tried to think if she recognized either of the men, but she didn't. "Who are you, and why am I here?" She should be scared, but figured if they wanted her dead, she would be ... right?

The idea of being dead sparked a vague memory of a monster attacking her. It flitted through her mind and her muscles tensed. She rubbed her abs, but she didn't feel any bandages.

The mean man's face hardened while the taller man just nodded and spoke. "I'm Steve, this here's Vernon. We saw you writing up a story on that tourist who had been attacked by a wild animal. We needed to talk with you about what you wrote before it got published. It occurred to us if you ...

well, if you understood us better, you could lean your writing accordingly."

Heat built in Paige's gut. "You kidnapped me to control what I wrote? Do you really think that that will work? I'm a journalist with integrity." Her mind whirled. Why would they care how she wrote up a story about a wild animal attack?

The brute, Vernon, sneered at her. "Oh, I believe you'll think twice before you write anything damning about what you saw. You see, it wasn't just any wild animal that attacked that tourist, it was a werewolf—" Paige jerked as if hit when she heard that word, but Vernon continued, unaware, or uncaring, "—and now that you're one of us, it isn't in your best interest to write about the wild animal attack and start a witch hunt ... so to speak."

Cold dread shot through her like an arrow. *Did he just say I was a werewolf? Is he mentally unstable? The other man, Steve, didn't even flinch at the word. Am I in a looney bin? Can I get away or am I locked in? Is there a story here? Would Dominik accept it if I wrote it?*

Paige slowly pushed herself up to a sitting position. "You think you're a werewolf? And you think that *I'm* a werewolf too?" She tried to keep her voice steady and calm. No reason to upset the crazies.

Vernon rolled his eyes. Steve's smile widened. "I

know it's a lot to take in. You've lived your whole life not believing in anything paranormal ... weird, and here we are trying to convince you that we're the normal ones. I was like that once. Vernon was born this way, I wasn't. Like you, I was bitten. It's probably why he's more powerful than either of us. I don't really know, though."

"Uh-huh. Okay. Sure." Paige slowly nodded at the crazy man. She held eye-contact and kept a small smile on her face. She tried to remember the lifeguard training on how to deal with unstable patrons.

Vernon shot up. "I can feel her mocking us. I never knew how much more information you got as pack alpha. We can't do this the slow way; she's pissing me off too much. That or I have to leave, but there isn't anyone else I trust to do this."

Steve's face scrunched up. "Okay, yeah. You shift, I'll stay like this to explain what's going on. You're too wound up to be gentle with her. Can you feel it? She's going to be submissive. Probably good for the pack, but not good until she finally makes her first shift. I can't believe the other submissives left after ... never mind, just shift."

Paige didn't know what they were talking about. She decided she needed to go find some werewolf books from the library. Would this place have a library? She needed to find out who was in charge and ask them. *How long am I here for? Why am I here? What did I do to end up in this place? I need something to explain this if I'm going to be stuck with these delusional people.*

Before she could stop it, Vernon began to strip off his clothes, then his body ... did ... something. *Gah! What the hell is happening to him? Bodies are not supposed to do that!*

It didn't take long for Vernon to go from a bully of a man to a large gray wolf with black paws. Terrified, Paige backed up against the wall and gaped at the wolf. "What ... did you give me drugs? Am I sleeping? Is this a nightmare? How?"

Steve stood and approached the bed. "No, Paige, this isn't a dream. It's real. You're a werewolf, like us. We brought you into our pack to help with our public relations. You can't write about random animal attacks for that paper of yours. The other packs will know what you're writing about, and we'll get in trouble. We need you to fix this, so they don't think it's because of a werewolf."

Paige's fear morphed into anger. "You're telling me you tried to kill me, made me into a monster like you, so you could use me? What the hell is wrong with you? God above! Can I leave now?"

Steve's face hardened. "You can't leave yet. We need to make sure you understand more about what it means to be a werewolf and in a pack. You have to understand you're part of our family now.

This room is yours."

"So, you've kidnapped me?"

"Of course not. You can still go to work, head home during the days as you need, but we want you to be part of the pack until you feel the connection." He reached into a bag by the door. "Look, I even have a welcome gift for you." He handed her a bottle of garlic salt with a fancy label. "My family produces this. It's the best you'll find anywhere."

She felt like she'd been punched. "Can I please just go home now?"

His face flattened. "Maybe tomorrow."

CHAPTER 5 - 4 O'CLOCK HAPPY HOUR!

Tamsin gazed at the stack of short stories her students had handed in after a weekend of writing. She enjoyed teaching this class, and for the most part, the creations were fun to read. Of the twenty-odd papers that were turned in, there would be a few that hurt her head and sensibilities. She stacked and put the papers in her shoulder satchel and headed out to her car.

Without anyone scheduled to train at the gym, she should go home and start grading all the stories;

it would be the smart move. However, as a teacher, hitting the bar at four on a Monday was totally understandable, acceptable even. Alcohol didn't mess up werewolves as much as it did normal humans. She could go, have a few beers to take the edge off her day, and then go home and see what wonders her students had gifted her.

She headed to Over the Rainbow, a gay tavern and grill in her neighborhood. She slid into a stool at the bar and ordered a tap beer. Being as early as it was, she was the only one there. The bartender, Antonio, wearing a rainbow-striped tank top and tiny black shorts, sashayed over with her beer. "When are you taking me out on a date, beautiful?"

"You say that to all the customers, but you're just flirting with me because I'm the only one in here. Admit it, you prefer flirting with the men."

Leaning in close, his loose black curls falling forward, the gorgeous man winked. "Not true, I like all the sexy people. I only want to eat ... with the ones I fantasize about. One of these days you'll say yes and make my night."

With a smile, Tamsin lifted her beer in salute. "Here's to dreaming." She drank the beer down in one go, the speed letting her muscles relax. The banter lifted her spirits, and she smiled at the man whose face was mere inches from hers.

Antonio licked his lips. "Does this mean you swing both ways, Tamsin? I only see you watching other women when the place is full." He winked at her then asked, "Do you want another one?"

Tamsin wanted something, but she wasn't sure if beer would fit the bill. Heat spread from her belly outward, and she barely stopped herself from leaning forward. With a sigh, she shut her eyes. "Yes, another one, please."

As Antonio flipped around to get the beer, Tamsin thought about the last time she'd given in to her needs. Being a werewolf, she only let herself date other wolves. It made everything easier. She didn't like one-night stands, as much as her body craved it. It had been ... too long. And though she'd been with men a few times, she really did prefer women.

She finished her second beer and headed home. As she walked through the door of her third-floor walkup, her phone rang. Looking at the display, she saw a number she didn't recognize. The area code was Santa Cruz. Was it something to do with Aunt Elinore? On impulse, she answered.

"Hello?"

"Hi, I'm looking for Tamsin Hath."

"Can I ask who's calling?"

"This is Officer Rey Summers from the Santa Cruz police department. I'm calling to inform you of the passing of a relative of yours. An Elinore Hath."

The world dropped out from under her. "What happened?"

"At this point, we don't know."

"Do you need me to come out there?"

"It isn't a requirement, but you're her only living relative. Someone will need to handle her material stuff."

Trembling, Tamsin fell into a chair. "I'm going to come out. When can I see her?"

"That's hard to say. You don't have to see her body, it really isn't needed. Right now, we don't suspect foul play." The officer sounded distracted.

"I would like to see the body, preferably before any embalming or autopsy."

"Oh, well, I'll have to make some calls. If you could contact me when you get into town, I'll see what I can do."

Once she got off the phone, Tamsin began to shake. Anger surged through her. She knew it had to be Vernon or Steve cleaning up loose ends. There was no reason to kill her aunt. She was a witch, not a werewolf, and posed no threat to them.

"Aunt Elinore, do you want me to do anything about Vernon?"

For a few minutes, all Tamsin heard were sniffles as her aunt tried to control her tears. Tamsin grabbed the box of tissues and wiped at her own eyes. She loved her Uncle Clyde and learning of his death was like a knife to her heart.

"No. Clyde had gotten sick last fall, as you knew. He had been debating stepping down. When you came next summer, he was going to discuss you taking over. Vernon and that snake, Steve just jumped the gun, smelling weakness and deciding it was time they took the reins. They won't be good leaders, Tamsin. I still think-"

"No. I left for a reason, Aunt Elinore. I'm not returning to the pack."

"Why not?"

Why not? The words still haunted her ...

She would go to Santa Cruz, figure out which of the snakes killed Aunt Elinore, and do what she should've done six months ago when they played their dominance game with her uncle. She massaged her temples thinking about setting substitute teacher plans for her time away. She knew she needed to pack and sell her aunt's house, try to prove Vernon and Steve killed her, and finally separate her life from California. None of that would be quick. Weeks ... she needed a few weeks.

She grabbed her laptop, looked for a flight out, and then began her plans to separate herself from Chicago for at least three weeks. Her principal seemed understanding but stressed. They'd find her a long-term sub.

Then Tamsin planned out her next encounter with the Pacific Pack. She needed to teach those mutts a lesson because, this time, they'd gone too far. As she planned, tears trailed warm paths down her cheeks. Aunt Elinore was the last of her living relatives. For all intents and purposes, she was alone now. Wiping her face, Tasmin threw herself into her work. She had to stay focused.

CHAPTER 6 - THE HITS KEEP COMING

After two days, Paige finally escaped the confines of the pack house and made it back to her job at the beach. The sun tried to peek out from the clouds, but the temperature couldn't warm the cool ocean waves.

Tuesday wasn't the most popular day for tourists to come swim in the cold waters. Two hardy families sat eating meals that Paige could smell from half a beach away. This ability to smell everything was new, and she didn't know what she thought about it. She could separate the scents of each of the individual people and if she focused, she could hear their conversations.

As she sat there, her head throbbed, and the ground began to tilt. Her stomach swirled with unease. Her first day back on the job, and she wondered if she could work around people. Did werewolves have to be solitary creatures? She thought Vernon worked at the fire station, and hadn't Steve said he worked at the library? Both of those jobs involved people. *Is it just me?*

Bile gathered at the back of her throat, and she knew she couldn't continue. Sliding down the ladder, she signaled the other lifeguard and headed to the locker room. She found her boss.

"Paige, you're white as a ghost. You okay?"

She shook her head. "I don't think so. I feel nauseous."

"Go, let me know when you're well. You're off the schedule for now."

She was glad the nicer of the two bosses had been in. The other one would've probably sent her back out to work the rest of her shift.

After getting into her street clothes, she trotted to her car and debated where to go. Her mind said back to the pack house. She needed to ask Vernon or Steve about what the hell was wrong with her.

They said they were her pack, her family, but to her, they were her attackers. *How can I trust people who did this to me? And didn't they kill that tourist? They really are monsters. Does this make me a monster, too?*

No, I need time to decompress and figure things out. Home, I need to go home.

It had only been a few days since she'd been home, but somehow her sanctuary felt foreign to her. The smell was off, the colors more vibrant, everything was just ... wrong.

She stood in her living room and her couch called to her. With a jerk of her head, she headed to the dining room and her computer. "Article. I owe Dominik an article."

She found an email from Officer Summers. She combined the notes from the police with what she remembered from her own time on the scene. Her notebook was long gone, destroyed by her new 'family.'

It didn't take her long to get a story written and sent off to her boss. No sooner had she clicked 'send' on her email than her phone rang again. She sighed when she saw the caller.

"Hi, Dominik. Saw my email?"

The sounds of the newsroom almost swallowed

up his words. "Sure did, kid. I'll read your piece in a moment, I'm sure it's great. I have a new story for you."

Feeling sick and knowing her limits, Paige shook her head. "Is it something someone else can take? I've been–"

Dominik interrupted her before she could finish her thought. "It's a follow-up to one of your last stories. My nose smells something good here. It came in over the weekend. Death seems natural, but I think it's something more. Check it out. Happened in your neighborhood. The wife of that man whose death you covered a few months back. Chuck, or Charlie ... "

"Clyde? Clyde Hath? Elinore Hath is dead?" Paige's body began to tremble. The Haths lived next door to her. Her article six months ago had been so personal because she'd known the couple. When she'd moved to Santa Cruz, they'd welcomed her to the neighborhood, cooked her dinner and told her about the lay of the land. They were an older couple but welcoming of a younger neighbor.

When Clyde had died, she felt like a member of her own family had died, not that she had anyone to call family. Now Elinore was gone? She wondered if they had family to help close up their home. They never spoke about having any kids or anyone close to them. Despite all the dinners they'd cooked for her, they never spoke much about themselves. The more Paige thought about it, the stranger it seemed.

A tear dripped down her cheek. "Are you still with me, Paige?"

"What? Sorry, I must be in a dead zone. Can you repeat that?"

A grunt of annoyance. "Yeah, that man's wife is dead. Go down to the police station, find out what you can, and maybe get to the morgue. I want a write-up about this. See if you can connect it to the story you just sent me. If not, see if there was foul play involved. There's something big here. I can taste it, my girl."

Paige feared her editor's nose for a story wasn't wrong. "Right, I'm on it."

Hanging up the phone, a knot of fear twisted in her gut. Connecting these stories could mean her own life ... for real this time.

Chapter 7 - Home Sweet Home

Tamsin finished the last of the students' stories and placed the stack in her bag. The plane should be landing in San Francisco soon, and she could scan them in and send them to her principal to give to the long-term sub. She felt bad that she hadn't finished them and given them back before leaving Chicago, but she'd packed and left right away. Grading papers wasn't top of her to-do list. Writing up three weeks' worth of plans for her four preps had been.

After she bought the plane tickets and started making arrangements for her classes, she'd looked up the number for each of her clients to explain she'd be out of town. There were other personal trainers in town they could see while she was away. She knew she'd lose some of her regulars. She just hoped she'd get some of them back when she returned and wouldn't have to start completely over.

Nolan had offered to come with her. The pack wolf didn't know anything more than her aunt had died, but her uncle had died less than a year ago, and in werewolf society, that could only spell trouble. Tamsin refused, again not wanting the local pack to learn too much about her.

Tamsin watched out the small window as the plane approached the San Francisco airport. She always loved how it appeared like the plane would land on the water of the bay right before they landed on the tarmac. After collecting her bag, she rented a car and headed south down the coast to her aunt's house.

The house hadn't changed. Why had she thought it would?

The main floor had an open floor plan with an immense living room, dining room, and kitchen. The kitchen was large enough to feed a coven while brewing spells. She had another storage space in the basement for brewing scarier spells. The other half of the main floor held the master suit with a huge modern bedroom, walk in closet, and colossal bathroom.

The second floor had four bedrooms and three bathrooms. One of the rooms had been Tamsin's whenever she visited and she had stored some clothes there. Despite being 'her' room, all four rooms were used as guest rooms.

She put water in the kettle to boil as she circled the main floor.

Before she left Chicago, the lawyer that had been helping Aunt Elinore with her uncle's end-of-life dealings left her a message. Now that she was in Santa Cruz, she gave the man a call.

"Gold, Rothen, and Cinder Law Firm, how can I help you?" A cheerful voice assaulted her ear as Tamsin dropped onto the couch in the living room. She'd left her Chicago apartment at five-thirty in the morning and was in no mood for chipper.

"I'd like to speak with Philip Gold." She tried not to snarl.

"Is he expecting your call?"

"I'm not sure. He left me a message to call him about Clyde and Elinor Hath." *Do I sound as stressed to her as I do to myself? Keep it civil.*

"If you'll give me your name, I'll see if he's available."

She bit back a sigh. "Please let him know Tamsin Hath is calling about Elinor Hath's death and the transfer of executorship of Clyde Hath's estate." *There, I sounded official and everything. I can do this.*

The line went silent for a moment. "I'm sorry for your loss. I'll let him know right away, Ms. Hath." The excitement in her voice was replaced with somber respect. Tamsin wasn't sure which she preferred. She started to understand why her aunt bristled whenever she asked how she had been doing.

After a few moments, an older male voice clicked over. "Ms. Hath, it's Philip Gold. I'm glad you made it to Santa Cruz, though I'm sorry for the reason. I'm very busy this week but have time on Friday at one. Could you come down to my office then? I'll have a lot of paperwork seeing as we have two people to work through."

Tamsin rubbed her forehead, wishing she didn't have to do any of it. "Yeah, that sounds fine. I'll be there then."

She got up to make her tea before she made her next call to the local police. It took her a few transfers to get to Officer Summers. "Is there any chance I can see my aunt's body today?"

"I'm sorry, Ms. Hath, things are busy, and I'll need to be there. The earliest I can get you in is Friday morning. Would that work?"

She sighed but knew fighting red tape was beyond tooth and claw. "Thank you for any help you can give, Officer."

After Tamsin finished her tea, she decided she needed something stronger to drink. She had one more call to make before she could relax. She found beer in the fridge, a local brew, Colossal Claude, which surprised her. She didn't think it was something her aunt drank.

She drank the bottle quickly then dialed the number to the local pack. She knew in her gut they were to blame, but until she could see them, talk to them, hear their words face to face, she wouldn't have her proof. Just cause to take the scoundrels out.

"Tamsin, is that you? What are you calling about?" Vernon sounded defensive.

Her hand tightened, and she dropped the bottle in the recycling bin before it cracked. "Vernon. I'm just calling to let you know I'm in Santa Cruz. A respectful check-in as a lone wolf. I'm hoping to talk with you in the next few days."

"Here? In town?" Did the alpha sound surprised? "What are you doing all the way out here? Don't you live in Chicago now? Something wrong with your aunt?"

Just hearing his voice made her shiver. Deciding desperate times called for desperate measures, Tamsin grabbed a mug and poured some whiskey into it. She took a sip.

"Don't talk to me about my family after what you did." Her voice slithered out of her, a low snarl. She wanted to climb through the phone and throttle the damn upstart.

"Whoa, calm down, Tam. That was a legal dominance fight."

Tamsin saw red. "It's *Tamsin*, and you know it. And if that's all it was, what happened to my aunt?"

"What are you talking about?" Again, confusion.

"I think you know what I'm talking about. She's dead, Vernon. I'm here to find out why." Every word had come out as a snarl. It had been years since she couldn't mask the anger in her voice. She threw back the rest of her drink, but rage still surged through her. Jaw clenched, a crack was the only warning she had before the mug shattered in her grip. She dropped the bloody pieces in the sink and turned on the water to rinse away any slivers.

When was the last time I was so emotional? Tears fell again as she fought for control.

"And you think it was me? Us? Why would we do that? She's no werewolf, no threat. I've heard there's a black witch coven that recently moved into town, it could've been them. Look, how about this. We have a new wolf in the pack, a reporter. She's real good at figuring things out. I'll have her help you search."

Tamsin took a few calming breaths. Her mind swirled as the ground tilted under her. The pack hadn't killed her aunt? Could it have been natural causes? Could it have been something else? "I don't need one of your new wolves, Vernon."

A grunt. "Please, look, I know we've had some issues between us in the past. Just let my wolf help you. She's a good sort. It will make me feel better knowing we, the pack, helped you figure this out."

There was silence as Tamsin tried to think of a way to tell Vernon and the pack to take a long walk off a short pier. It really wasn't the whole pack Tamsin didn't like, just Vernon and Steve, the two out-of-town leaders who'd come in and taken over after her dad had died. And made things worse.

"The pack is your lifeline, your family. They'll always be there for you, Tam. Don't overlook the power of connection and what it can bring you."

"But, Dad, I'm strong. I can do things on my own."

"You can, dear, but why? If you can use the pack, why separate yourself?"

"Look, Tamsin," Vernon's voice pulled her from her musings of her dad. "I'm not taking no for an answer. Her name is Paige. Paige Glass. I'll text her contact information over to you. Use her. Again, she's good at what she does. She can help you."

Every one of Tamsin's instincts told her to walk away from this help, but a niggling bit of her thought that having a connection to the pack meant she could keep an eye on them. If Vernon was pushing his kid so hard, she was probably one of his cronies. Tamsin could get some inside information if she played her cards right. "Fine, I'll give her a chance, but if she's an idiot, I'm not keeping her around. You know I don't suffer fools."

CHAPTER 8 - TRUST ISSUES

Paige checked her email one more time. Officer Summers hadn't gotten back to her about Elinore's death. She wasn't surprised. The fried rice and Mongolian beef from her favorite hole-in-the-wall local Chinese restaurant didn't quite fill the void in her belly. She'd never been so hungry. She'd skipped lunch, feeling nauseous from her lifeguard job, and now felt ravenous.

Her phone on the table next to her vibrated.

Flipping it over, she debated answering it. She guessed her new 'family' wanted to know where she was and why she wasn't 'home' yet. As a product of the foster care system, she'd never had such doting parents before, and she'd always been jealous of kids who did. Now she decided she preferred the freedom to do as she wanted.

Rolling her eyes, she answered. "Paige here. Can I help you?"

"Hey P, Vernon. An old packmate just flew into town. Her aunt passed away. For some reason, she thought it was the pack, but I believe I convinced her it wasn't. She's hell-bent on finding the culprit. I know you love writing about crime, and thought you'd be willing to help her investigate. Anyway, I gave her your number."

"Uh, do I have a say in this?"

Vernon grunted. "You don't want to help this person? Her aunt just died. I thought you were a nice lady."

Paige's head dropped into her hand. "It's not that. I just don't know her. Hell, I don't know you. I have two jobs and ... " How could she tell this stranger what was going on around her? *How can I help anyone when I can't even get through a day at the beach without wanting to puke?*

"It'll be fine. Tamsin probably won't ask for much. Just be there so she knows the pack wasn't responsible for her aunt's death."

Paige's mind came to a screeching halt. "Was the pack responsible? You killed that tourist and attacked me. Is it such a stretch to think you killed this woman, too?" She couldn't quite believe she'd been so bold, but she had to know.

Vernon sighed. "I didn't kill her. Why would the pack kill a non-werewolf?"

"She found out about werewolves, and you were afraid she'd tell someone? Like that tourist?"

Another sigh could be heard over the line. "I just told you, her niece used to be part of the pack. I pretty much implied that she knew about us already. She wasn't a security risk."

Paige rubbed her temples and tried to put the pieces together. Too much new information had to find places in her mind. "Okay, not a security risk. Help this Tamsin person out to find the actual killer, if there was one. She could've just died of natural causes."

"That's right, good thinking."

Dread gripped her gut and twisted. "Who is the aunt?" Her voice barely came out as a whisper. She doubted a non-werewolf would've heard it. Her fork rattled against her plate. Letting go, she balled her fists and shut her eyes as she waited for the answer she knew was coming.

"Elinore Hath."

"Again?" Why was this happening to her? Her

neighbor, her job, her *pack*—ha!—and *she* had to combine them all. Paige missed the next few things Vernon said as her worlds collided.

"I'm sorry. Could you repeat that?"

Vernon grumbled. "What do you mean again?"

Paige thought back and realized she'd let that word slip out. "Oh, sorry, my boss at the paper asked me to do a story about her death, and now you with this. It seems odd that I'm being asked to investigate this woman's death by two different people, that's all."

"Hmm." There was a coldness to Vernon's response. "I assume when you write this story of yours, you'll remember to keep the pack's interest in the forefront of your mind."

What does that even mean? "Of course."

CHAPTER 9 - MAC AND CHEESE

After making her calls, Tamsin went up to her room, the only one with a private bathroom, and unpacked. She logged in to her computer and sent the student assignments to her principal. She found an update from the sub, which made her feel both better and guiltier about not being there for her students.

Her stomach began to twist from hunger; the meager ham and cheese sandwich she'd grabbed at the Chicago airport wasn't enough, and not eating wasn't smart. She headed back down to search the kitchen for food. Before she got down the stairs, a knock came at the door.

Answering it, she found a willowy woman, delicate, with strawberry blond curls that framed her face. The woman's bright green eyes gazed up at her, nervous but determined. Her lush mouth was tight, like she was prepared to argue. One sniff, and Tamsin knew this woman was a werewolf.

Tamsin raised an eyebrow and leaned on the edge of the door, blocking the way in. "Can I help you?"

The other person released a huff of air from her nose. "My name's Paige. I live next door and I knew your ... well, I knew Elinore. I knew Clyde as well. They were really nice people."

"Good for you, Paige. But that doesn't tell me why you're here." Tasmin leaned against the door jam, arms crossed, drumming her fingers against her bicep.

The woman's shoulders seemed to droop, and then she straightened. "Look, I don't really know why I'm here, but I'd like to help you. Your family were the only people I've known in years that I've cared about, and I don't know why either of them died, but if I *can* help, I really do want to. Vernon ... do you know him?"

A small growl escaped Tamsin as she gave a curt nod.

Paige laughed. "You seem to have a similar opinion of the man as I do. Anyway, he asked me to help you. My first instinct is to do the opposite of anything he asks, but I want to know what happened to Elinore. But, in all honesty, I'm also a journalist, and my editor asked me to write the story about her death as well. You can look up the story I wrote on Clyde six months ago." She bit her lip, as if shocked at how many words she'd just said.

Tamsin could smell the sincerity. Standing face to face with a person, no one could lie to her, which was a benefit as a teacher. She was tired and hungry, and didn't want to work with any of the pack cronies, but this beautiful woman—where did that thought come from? This wolf intrigued her.

She stepped back. "Have you eaten dinner?"

Tamsin walked into the kitchen and searched to see what she could make. She found cheese and milk in the fridge, noodles and croutons in the cupboards. Cooking always relaxed and centered her. A glance over her shoulder showed Paige still standing on the stoop. "In or out, Paige."

"Oh, yeah, sorry." The door clicked shut. "Yeah, I've eaten. I don't care if you eat though. Thanks for letting me in. If you don't mind, your aunt stocks some beer that I like."

That explains the beer ... and gives a bit of credence to her story.

She grabbed two beers and started making mac

and cheese. "So, I talked to Vernon today. He told me about you, though not that you knew my family. He said you were new to the pack. What made you choose pack life?"

Paige snorted. "Choose, that's a funny way of putting it."

"You didn't choose to become a werewolf? How did this happen?" Tamsin waved her hand up and down, indicating Paige's body. "You don't just magically become a wolf."

The woman tipped back her beer, then glared at the bottle. "Is this the same beer? It's like I'm drinking juice."

"You're a werewolf, hon. Alcohol doesn't affect you the same way. Wait, what do you know about werewolves?"

Paige smacked the bottle to the counter. "What do I know?" Her voice rose a bit. "I was sitting and writing an article less than a week ago when a monster attacked me. I thought I was being eaten alive ... and then I passed out. I woke up and was told a mythical creature was real. Apparently, now *I'm* the monster. And now I'm sitting in the kitchen of one of my favorite people, and she's dead. And, for some reason, I can't get drunk."

"It's been less than a week? And you didn't know about werewolves before you were attacked?

Who?" Tamsin got lost in her cooking and didn't realize she hadn't asked a full question until she heard Paige's response.

"Who attacked me? Vernon? Wait, no, it couldn't be him. He showed me his wolf form, and the monster that attacked me was bigger. I don't actually know. It was dark and by the time I saw it, the beast was chewing on my gut, so sorry if my report lacks crucial details."

Tamsin searched above in the upper cupboards until she found the brandy. She poured a bit into a glass. "This will help. It isn't that you *can't* get drunk, it's just more difficult. And harder liquor helps."

Paige slammed back the amber liquid, a shudder traveling down her body. She visibly relaxed.

Tamsin considered Paige. If it was a big wolf ... . "So, Steve attacked you, turned you, and you weren't consulted first. That's ... new." The thought of turning someone without their consent irked Tamsin. Anger surged through her. *These assholes are out of control!*

She filled Paige's glass with more brandy, which she quickly drank.

Paige's head slowly swung up from her now empty glass, eyes slightly unfocused. "Not normal?"

The drunk wolf in her kitchen made Tamsin snicker. "Each pack defines what is normal for their pack. I can't say what's normal for this pack anymore. I can tell you how my dad ran it, even how my uncle ran things, but Vernon has obviously changed protocols. Being a lone wolf, I don't know how things are run now."

"What's a lone wolf?"

"A wolf not associated with a pack."

"But your dad used to run this pack, so you weren't always a lone wolf, right?"

Tamsin turned on the oven light to see how much longer the food would take. Her stomach growled, demanding recognition. "I was born a werewolf, not bitten like you. My mom and dad were also born werewolves. When I was a teen, Vernon and Steve came here from Texas. Vernon, like me, was born a wolf, but Steve had been bitten. Too young if you ask me."

Paige tilted her head. "Too young? Another rule? Or is this one of your dad's rules?"

"Dad always thought that new wolves shouldn't be turned until after a person was fully formed. So, usually in their twenties. Vernon bit Steve when he was fourteen. Really young for a new wolf. Vernon's pack kicked him out, and for some reason, they ended up here."

"Could your dad have kicked them out?" Despite her mostly clear words, Paige tilted in her seat.

Tamsin shrugged. "Other packs did. At least,

that was part of their sob story. Anyway, my mom died after I graduated from college. My dad didn't want to live without her. My uncle took over. He was dominant ... but not more dominant than me. I could've stayed, but it was hard having any other alpha than my dad."

"I know you have every right to be alpha, Tam, but I've always dreamed of leading our family's pack."

I bit my lip, every part of my being knowing I was the rightful alpha of the Pacific Pack. I was strong and had the power to lead. Moreover, I couldn't be submissive to Uncle Clyde, no matter how much I loved him.

I searched his face, then Aunt Elinore's. She was so proud of her husband. "You know, I'm young, and I've always wanted to travel. Maybe you taking over is best after all, Uncle Clyde."

Aunt Elinore beamed at me, and a small piece of my heart broke. Am I running from the pain of losing Mom and Dad?

No, of course not, I'm giving Uncle Clyde his chance. And really, I can live as a lone wolf ... right?

Tamsin bit back the memory. They were both gone now. She'd do anything to have them back. Back then, she'd run from the pain of losing both her parents, and now she's lost the last people who cared for her. She knew she was strong, yet she felt lost and alone in the world. *Buck up, Tamsin, you've a job to do!*

"I don't get this dominant thing. Am I dominant?" Paige bit her lip, brows coming together.

"No, you don't know how to tamp down your power. You're a submissive wolf."

"What does that mean?"

Tamsin sighs. "It means you don't feel the need to fight for position. You don't care if another wolf leads the pack. Other wolves will feel the need to protect you."

Paige picked up her empty glass and stared at it as if wondering where the liquor went. Tamsin smiled at Paige before tipping more brandy into the glass. "Be careful, friend. You can still get a hangover."

"Got it. So, I don't feel power from you. Are you submissive? Wait, you just said you weren't." She glared at her glass as if it were the reason she was making mistakes, then brought it up to her mouth and her pretty lips. *Focus, Tamsin, do not think of her lips!*

Tamsin watched as Paige sipped from her glass and put it down. Then Tamsin dropped all her walls. Her power filled the room like a cool ocean. Paige froze in her seat, eyes widening, her breathing stopped. After a few seconds, Tamsin put her blocks back in place, reeling in her alpha presence. "Does that answer your question?"

Paige gulped in some air. "Can all wolves do that?"

"No. Most can't. Only the very powerful. It's why I can't be in most packs, and why I left the pack to my uncle. If I'm not alpha, then I'd get in the way of the alpha."

The oven timer rang. Tamsin put on oven mitts, grabbed the pan, and set it on the stove. A new wolf never understood their eating needs. She scooped hot, gooey mac and cheese onto two plates and placed one in front of Paige.

"Wait, I already ate," she protested.

"Then don't have any. I made enough, so it's fine if you change your mind."

As she took her first bites of food in hours, Paige tasted her serving. The woman's eyes widened, and she groaned before tucking in. She swallowed a bite and said, "You can cook! Did you learn from Elinore? I haven't had a home-cooked meal since the last time she cooked for me." She paused. "Oh, God, I'm sorry, that was rude."

Tamsin smiled at Paige. "No, it's fine. I'm glad she had you to spoil. She talked about a neighbor kid she fed. She never named you, just said it was someone I'd like."

"You know I'm not a kid, right?"

"Sorry, you look at most eighteen, and she called everyone a kid."

"I'm thirty."

Tamsin laughed. "Well, old lady, I guess I'll have to take care of you, then. You're a full year older than me."

CHAPTER 10 - THE WAY TO HER HEART ...

Paige wasn't sure if she'd ever eaten mac and cheese that tasted so delicious. She also never knew watching a woman move around a kitchen cooking could be so alluring. Or was it because Tamsin was a few inches taller than Paige with dark hair—and was there a bit of red in her hair? She'd need to see it in the sun to see if it were dark brown or auburn. Her eyes seemed to match the mystifying hair color.

As she moved in the kitchen, Paige saw the loose blouse tighten over muscular arms. She could tell Tamsin hid strength under her button-down shirt. *I bet she works out regularly. Or maybe that was a byproduct of being a wolf ... or being a powerful wolf. Vernon has lots of muscles too. If it's only the powerful wolves, there's no hope for me. I'll stay rail thin.*

Another groan escaped Paige as she ate the food she'd said she didn't want. Maybe Tamsin wouldn't notice.

"So, you're a lone wolf. Could I be a lone wolf?"

A small smile graced Tamsin's face when Paige had looked up. *What is she thinking? Did I say something wrong?*

"Technically, you can be a lone wolf, but there are some issues. First of all, you live in a city with a pack. It's hard to coexist with a pack as a lone wolf."

"Do you live in a city with a pack?"

She snorted. "I do. I live in Chicago, and living with that pack in town is hard. They dictated the places I can run as a wolf, live as a human, locations I can work. I accepted their rules because I'm living in their territory."

Paige dropped her fork. "You let them define your life that much?"

The sexy wolf ... er, strong wolf shrugged. "It's the life of the lone wolf." She took a bite of food.

"The next thing is, you're submissive. The longer you're a werewolf, the more you're going to realize you crave touch and contact with other wolves. You need it more as a submissive wolf. It's hard to resist."

Paige thought about that. "How long have you lived as a lone wolf? How do you combat that need?"

Tamsin slumped. "I have two jobs. I teach, and I'm a personal trainer. As a teacher, I have an excuse to interact with students for nine months. It isn't physical, but it meets a social need. As a personal trainer, I get one-on-one interactions. It isn't perfect, but it helps. I was going to spend the summer here with Aunt Elinore."

"But what about ... more? Do you date?"

After a moment of pregnant silence, they both took a few bites of dinner. Tamsin sipped her beer. "Is writing for the paper your only job?"

Paige let the subject change slide. "I'm also a lifeguard at the beach."

"Sounds fun."

Leaning back, Paige pursed her lips. "Can I ask you a question? I thought about asking Vernon or Steve, but I'm really not comfortable with them."

"You can ask, but I'm not promising any answers."

"Fair. Since I was attacked–"

"Bitten."

"What?"

Tamsin sighed. "I know you were attacked, but generally we just say 'bitten' when describing the transformation. It's less," she waved her hands, "triggering."

"Ah, fine. Okay. Since I was *bitten*, I've only been back to work at the beach once. It was horrible. I thought I was going to be sick. The people ... I could smell them and hear everything they said. And all their food, too. I got dizzy and nauseous." Her hand covered her mouth just thinking about it.

"If you throw up my food, I'm never cooking for you again."

Paige's eyes widened and snapped her focus up to Tamsin's eyes. The other woman was laughing at her. "You're teasing me?"

"Well, I don't know. Don't test me on this. So, they sent you out without *any* training?"

Paige tilted her head. "Training? What type of training?"

"Well, tell me, what do you smell now?"

Lifting her head, Paige sniffed. She could smell the tantalizing scent of Tamsin, but she wasn't sure how to describe that, so she set it aside. "There's the cheese and pasta, which is so much *more* than any other mac and cheese I've ever smelled. I think I can smell three ... or is it four different cheeses?"

"Five. But not bad."

"I can smell the candles Elinore always burned at dinner and ... I don't know, something else that reminds me of her ... does that make sense?"

Tamsin smiled, her face softening. "It does." She rubbed her face with her elegant-looking hands. "There's a way to block out all the information your newly enhanced senses are taking in. More than that, you're stronger, probably run faster. There are a lot of changes happening to you. The pack should be training you. How many pack members have you met?"

"Pack ... members? Like Vernon and Steve?"

"I mean more than them. Last I checked the pack had ten or twelve members. It's been several years; people move in and out, but two people do not a pack make."

Paige looked down and realized she'd eaten all of the mac and cheese she'd been served. She sipped at her brandy and sighed contentedly. "I've only met the two. They kept saying 'family,' but I never met more than the two of them. Now that you mention it, that's strange. So, besides learning how to block out my super powers of strength and smell, anything else I should know about?"

Tamsin watched Paige for a minute. "Do you want any more food?" She got up and filled her own plate.

Paige knew she'd eaten enough but couldn't resist. "Yes, please."

Tamsin looked pleased as she scooped more onto both their plates. "When you came over, you told me you didn't like Vernon or Steve. I knew you hadn't lied to me because I can smell a lie. I'm going to ask Vernon, to his face, if he killed Elinore."

"You can smell a lie?"

"Usually. Some people can cover it up; usually they're psychopaths. They tend to lie so much that anything they say sounds like the truth. Vernon, for all his faults, is a straight shooter. I should be able to smell the truth or lie of what he says."

Paige bit her lip. "Do you really think he killed Elinore?"

Tamsin sighed. "I don't know anymore. I was convinced of it when I left home this morning, but he sounded shocked that she was dead. He asked that I utilize you to help me get to the bottom of her death. Not only because you were pack, but he said you were good at finding the truth. Neither of these sounds like the words of a guilty man."

"So, do you think *I* can smell the lie someone tells me? As a reporter that would be excellent."

Tamsin ate a bit more food, watching Paige. She'd softened her gaze a lot from the person who'd answered the door. "Probably not today; have you even wolfed out yet? But eventually even the newest of wolves learns the tricks."

Paige's heart pounded in her chest like a sledgehammer. "Wolfed out?"

Chapter 11 - Reality Check

Tamsin picked up the plates and moved them to the sink. She searched for something to cover the rest of the food so she could store it in the fridge.

A glance over her shoulder informed her Paige hadn't budged. "You do know you're going to become a wolf, and it won't be in the too-far-off future, right?"

"I'm going ... wolf ... become ... right." Paige

grabbed for her glass, and she threw back whatever was left of her drink.

Tamsin grinned. She was so cute. "You forgot about that, or hadn't thought about it?"

Paige rubbed her face. "If I'm honest, I hadn't thought about it. It's only been a few days, and I've been in denial most of that time. None of this really seems real yet. Werewolves? Really? Like, how are they real?"

"You said Vernon shifted."

"Yes, so I know they're real. And they didn't let me leave until my brain really got around it, but, like, how do you know *I'm* a wolf?"

Tamsin came around and sat on a stool next to Paige. Their thighs touched. Touch helped soothe the beast. "First of all, I can smell it on you. Close your eyes and smell me."

"Tam, your most important tool is sitting in the center of your face."

I crossed my eyes and stuck my tongue out at Dad. He laughed. I loved to hear him laugh. He was always so serious with the pack when training, but when it was just us, he was relaxed and goofy.

I focused on him and took a big sniff. My first

shift to werewolf had only happened two weeks ago, and everything was so new to me. I couldn't believe how everything had changed. "Eww! Dad! Did you just fart?"

Paige's eyebrows shot up before she snorted out a laugh. "Is that a pick-up line?"

"Not this time. For now, it's just training." Tamsin tried to ignore how Paige's question caused heat to build in her gut. If the submissive wolf didn't watch out, she just may pounce on her yet, new wolf or not. The sound of sniffing brought her back to the task at hand.

Paige's brow crinkled. "I smell something earthy? Maybe fur? Does that make sense?"

Tamsin knocked her shoulder into Paige. "Good work. You're smelling the wolf in me. If you were around humans—not that we aren't human; we're just a bit more—you wouldn't smell that."

"Can you teach me how to block everything, too?"

"I can. I used to help my dad with training. But not right now. It's late and I'm tired. I have to find out who else may have been after my aunt, if not the wolves."

Paige watched her for a moment before asking,

"Who do you think it could be?"

"Well, I don't know, that's the question. I need to see the body, talk to the police, talk to the lawyer, talk with Vernon ... and find the witches."

Paige froze next to her. "The what now?"

"Well, you know there are werewolves; is it such a stretch that there are witches as well? Vernon said a coven of black witches moved into town and that they may be trying to eliminate the competition."

"There are witches, and werewolves, and vampires?"

"Oh, my!"

Paige glared at her, and Tamsin laughed. She was liking this snarky lady more and more. "No, only werewolves and witches, from what I've run into. If there is anything else in our big bad world, I've neither seen nor smelled them."

The willowy woman shivered. "All of this is hurting my head. I've never even read paranormal books with werewolves."

Tamsin leaned in and whispered. "I *could* recommend some. They wouldn't tell you much of anything factual, but the naughty scenes are fantastic."

Paige blushed the color of a ripe tomato.

Tamsin stood. "I need to clean up the kitchen and get some sleep. Where I come from, it's two hours later. I'll adjust eventually, but right now I'm tired."

"I could help you with that. You cooked, I'll clean. It's the rules."

"Are you sober enough not to break anything?"

Tamsin watched Paige stand. She swayed for a moment then shook her head. "I'll be fine. Once I'm at the sink, I can lean on the counter and wash the plates."

With a chuckle, Tasmin smiled wide. "We have a dishwasher; no reason to do that. Why don't you sit on the couch until you can walk without tipping over? I wouldn't want you sleeping in the bushes."

Tamsin helped Paige to the couch, then filled glasses with water for both of them. She sat down next to her.

Paige smiled. "So, what do you teach?"

"English. I get to inspire teenagers to write, and then I'm forced to read the words with which they attack me. It's invigorating."

Paige laughed. "I remember the days in which teachers forced specific types of writing on us. I used to try and challenge the assignment to the edge of what was allowed. I remember arguing about the parameters of the assignment when I got a low grade."

"Gah! You're one of those! You also erased the board after class."

Paige grinned wider. "Every day. My creative

writing teacher was dreamy."

Tamsin let her head fall back. "That is so wrong on so many levels. He was probably too old for you, and that would make you jailbait. Students just don't think about those things. Not to mention, from the teacher's side, students are just so *young* looking. Give me a beautiful ... er never mind."

Paige sipped her water. "Hmmm, beautiful, eh. Why do you assume my creative writing teacher was a man?" She slid her hand to Tamsin's leg, then jerked it away, and shot up. "I should head home. Apparently, alcohol does affect me, and I'm going to regret things in the morning. Good night ... " She shook her head as if stopping herself from saying something. "Tamsin." Walking slowly, Paige headed for the door.

CHAPTER 12 – THERE ARE MORE?

Paige woke up, head throbbing, and grabbed the water on the bedside table. Thankfully, the room wasn't spinning. Considering the night before, she was glad she'd had enough food to balance the alcohol she'd drunk.

Sitting up, she wrapped her arms around her legs and thought about the previous night. *Did I really put my hand on Tamsin's leg? Did I really flirt with that sexy lady? Gah! No more alcohol. She's gorgeous, but she's leaving town, and grieving. Why would she want anything to do with me? Not only am I a stranger, I remind her of the pack she obviously loathes.*

Paige had learned a lot about Tamsin and potentially the case she needed to get writing about. *I could call Vernon and check in like a good pack stooge. Screw that. What has he done to earn my loyalty? Attacked me, or let Steve attack me. Not told me anything I need to know to function with these new senses. He even threw me to a lone wolf, gah! What was that all about? What is the real reason he wants me to work with Tamsin? Does he think Tamsin will attack me and finish what Steve started? Maybe Tamsin has an idea of the alpha's rationale ... am I brave enough to ask?*

Fidgeting with her phone, she finally punched in a number.

"Coming in today?" The voice on the other end was gruff and sounded distracted.

"No. I'm going to take the rest of the week off. I'm not getting better, and I don't want to get anyone at the beach sick. I'm not sure I'm up to running into the water if anyone needs saving."

"This doesn't look good, Paige. Call on Saturday, or you could lose your job." The line went dead before she could say anything back. She'd known other lifeguards who'd lost their jobs when they couldn't make it in. *I guess they'd prefer getting the tourists sick, or endangering their lives to a lifeguard who may not be able to perform their duties.*

She debated her computer in the dining room. Should she take the day to write? She had notes she needed to organize, or maybe write an outline for a new book. She seemed to have a new concept fall into her lap.

Again, her mind flitted to the house next door and the attractive woman who'd gotten her drunk. Maybe she could help Tamsin. The lone wolf didn't seem to need help; she had all her ducks in a row, and then some ... but you never knew. Maybe having another set of eyes to check things out would be welcome.

No, she wasn't going to throw herself at a woman who obviously didn't need her. Tamsin saw her as the Pacific Pack's crony, and she couldn't blame her.

Unfolding herself from her bed, Paige showered and dressed in jeans and a t-shirt, and headed to the kitchen. Her stomach let her know that skipping breakfast wasn't an option. She brewed coffee, threw a bagel in the toaster, took out peanut butter and milk, and was ready for as much cooking as she felt capable of.

Maybe I should watch cooking shows or get a cookbook. I'm thirty years old. I should be able to do more than toast a bagel and brew coffee ... right?

Breakfast done, she sat down at her computer. She started with email. Nothing in from Officer Summers. She wasn't surprised; it was still early. She'd try calling later in the day. From there she began typing up notes on Elinore's death. As she thought about everything she knew, her work progressed slowly and emotionally. Searching old records, she thought about trying to cross reference her article with Clyde's but wasn't sure how much she could before she got the official report for the police.

She rubbed her face, trying to figure out how to keep everything professional. Like the article she wrote on Clyde, she knew a bit of herself may seep in.

She brought her plate into the kitchen and poured herself a second cup of coffee. Her phone vibrated. She checked the display. The area code said it was a Chicago number. She debated ignoring it, but then she remembered.

"Hello?"

"Hi, Paige, it's Tamsin. When I contacted Vernon yesterday, he gave me your number. Is it okay that I'm calling?"

Warmth filled her, and she squeezed her eyes shut. She told herself there was no reason to be excited to hear this woman's voice. "Yeah, sure. But

I have your number now. You know that could be dangerous, right?" She couldn't help playing. "You're the only one who's answered any of my questions. You're in for it, now."

A warm laugh. Paige felt it to her toes. "Well, then it's good you have my number. Being untrained isn't wise. Call anytime you have a question." She wanted to ask if she could ask *any* question, but she wasn't quite that bold. Tamsin continued. "Anyway, I'm going to head out to face Vernon this morning, ask him some questions. Want to tag along?"

The thought of Vernon seeing the two together as a joint front thrilled Paige. The thought of the two of them *being* a joint front thrilled her even more. She felt giddy. "Yeah, sounds great. I have some coffee made, want some?"

There was a pause and then, "If you have a travel mug, sure. A splash of cream or milk would be perfect. I'll be outside your place in ten minutes."

Paige saved her work and shut down her computer. She filled two travel mugs with coffee and headed out to meet Tamsin. She handed Tamsin the coffee, climbed in the SUV rental, branded with stickers, and they were off.

Tamsin smiled. "You look like you survived the night. Thanks for the coffee."

"Not a problem. It's my specialty. That, and toast."

"Ah, so you're a big fan of cooking?"

Paige snorted. "Growing up, none of the homes I lived in allowed any of us kids to do anything in the kitchen that could lead to burning down the house. I've debated trying to learn, but it's never been a priority."

After a sip of coffee, Tamsin darted a look to Paige before watching the road. "Sorry if this is getting too personal. I didn't know."

"No, it's okay. Being brought up in the foster system is just a piece of who I am. I don't mind. I really should learn how to cook." She smirked at Tamsin. "Maybe you could teach me."

Tamsin huffed. "Maybe. If after this meeting you still think it's a good idea, you can cook me fish tacos for dinner."

Paige froze, then her jaw dropped. Slowly, she shifted her gaze from the road to Tamsin's smirking face. Remembering how to breathe, she said, "I can't imagine you wanting food poisoning, but yeah, fish tacos tonight sounds great."

They pulled up beside a light-blue building near the beach. It looked like it had tons of rooms and could double as a bed and breakfast. This was a different place than Paige had been the previous weekend. She'd expected to go to the house where she'd stayed for her first few days as a werewolf.

Tamsin parked, seemingly secure in her knowledge of where they were. Paige followed slowly behind, less sure.

Come on, Paige. Tamsin is nice and seems to think these are good people ... they can't all be like Vernon and Steve ... can they?

CHAPTER 13 – THEY DON'T BITE ... HE'S AT WORK

Tamsin stomped up to the orange door of the house she grew up in. When her dad had been alpha, her family had lived in a suite of rooms in the back of the pack den. She tried not to think too hard about how empty the building felt. The last time she approached the building, the pack had fourteen pack members, with ten living in the den.

The only reason her uncle hadn't moved in was because a non-wolf couldn't live in the den house. Especially when that non-wolf was a witch.

She had Paige with her, so she didn't have to knock. Walking in, they entered into a large living room filled with couches, recliners, TVs, and tables. There were four people in the room. Tamsin recognized them all.

"But Mom, I'm ten. Why do I have to have babysitters? I'm old enough to take care of myself. Plus, I'm a werewolf!"

"Tamsin, you know you're not old enough to care for yourself, and Maria's your friend. The two of you will play some games, watch a movie, and eat pizza. What's wrong with that?"

"Yeah, squirt, I thought you liked hanging out with me?" Maria sauntered in from the kitchen, carrying two sodas. Mom didn't let me have soda. She said I was too young. Maria held up one of the cans. "Look, I brought you one, too."

Mom's eyes narrowed, but she pointedly spun on her heel and walked out of the pack house leaving me in Maria's care.

Maria Sanchez and Georgette Johnson sat on the couch farthest from the door. They were both in their mid-thirties and had often taken care of Tamsin when she was growing up. From what she remembered, they were both into computers and programming. On a closer sofa, she recognized Orin and Connie Jax, who were older than Maria and Georgette.

Maria leapt up and ran over to hug her. "Tamsin, I haven't seen you in ages. What are you doing here?"

Hugging her back, Tamsin felt like she was home. Her body tingled with its release of tension. "Maria, it's so good to see you." She pulled back, her body screaming for more. "I need to talk with Vernon or Steve."

Georgette, still sitting, whispered softly to herself, though Tamsin heard. "Did you bring us a submissive? Steve ran them all off."

Orin, the only man in the room, groaned. "Vernon is around. Steve, thankfully, is at work at the library."

Tamsin's eyebrow shot up. "Oh, you're not a fan?"

Orin narrowed his eyes. "We're it, Tamsin.

Everyone else has left. If it weren't for family and jobs, we would've left too. Vernon isn't horrible, but Steve ... gods above, he's awful, and Vernon lets him get away with just about anything."

Tamsin's heart stuttered. "You're it? What happened to everyone else?"

Connie leaned forward. "They left. Some when your uncle started losing control, but most in the last six months."

Georgette tilted to the left. "Who's that hiding behind you?"

Tamsin snorted. "This?" She reached back to slip her hand to Paige's back, guiding the woman forward. The contact caused shoots of electricity up her arm. "Why didn't you know you have a new wolf in your pack? She was bitten just a few days ago."

The quartet gaped. Maria got her mind working first. "We have a new pack member? We never met her. We never had the pre-biting training, or get to know you, or pre-biting ceremony, or–" Her voice rose, and she spoke faster and faster as the enormity of what happened hit them all.

Tamsin lightly placed her hands on her shoulders. "Slow down. You'll scare her. Steve attacked her. Paige didn't even know about werewolves. You are her pack. She hasn't been trained, and she doesn't know what's happening. The only 'family' she's met are her attackers. She needs to know there are good people in the pack."

Before anyone could say anything else, Vernon came into the room. "Tamsin, what are you doing here?"

Prowling towards him, Tamsin released her hold on her power. Even Vernon jerked at the slap. When they were barely a foot apart, she asked, "Did you kill my aunt?"

Gasps came from the other pack members in the room. They knew Aunt Elinore, and everyone who knew her, loved her.

Vernon's eyes narrowed, but with the power flowing, he couldn't refuse to answer. "As I told you on the phone yesterday, no, I didn't kill her. I think you should talk with the witches."

That wasn't a lie. What am I missing?

"Was my aunt's death connected to this pack?"

Vernon slumped. "No. We ... I ... had nothing against her."

Tamsin tamped down her power. She spun on her heel. "Paige, I'm going to head out. I have other things to do. I think you should stay here and meet your pack. You are welcome to make me dinner ... or not. Either way, text if you want me to pick you up or if one of these fine folks will drive you home."

Paige stopped breathing for a few seconds. "You want me to stay here? Okay, yeah, that makes sense. How about call after your next meeting and we can talk?"

Tamsin smiled. "Sure, but don't worry; they don't bite. That one's at work, and you survived it."

CHAPTER 14 – THROWN TO THE WOLVES

Paige sat in a large wooden chair with a padded seat and back. She was impressed with how comfortable it was. As large as the room was, with the oversized furniture and the framed pictures of scenery, an atmosphere of tranquility permeated the space. Despite that, the moment Tamsin left, she felt like she was at an interview for a job across from a panel of judges. At least Vernon had left, following out the sexy woman she'd just met. *Stop thinking of her like that. She probably sees you as an annoyance, nothing more.*

She bit her lower lip, gazing at the four older people in the room ... wolves? ... would that ever not be awkward? Tamsin seemed to like these people, but Paige still wanted to slink away, go home, and wake up from this nightmare.

The lady who'd hugged Tamsin spoke first. She sat across the room from her next to another woman. They both had brown hair. The speaker's brown eyes danced as she spoke, while the other woman seemed more pensive. "Hi, Paige, my name is Maria." She waved her thumb to the woman next to her. "This is Georgette and the couple over there are Orin and Connie. I know this is a lot, but we're all here to answer your questions. All of us have been part of the pack our whole life. Well, except for Connie. Like you, she didn't become a werewolf until later in her life."

Paige's apprehension morphed into frustration. These people had no idea. "Was she also attacked outside a dark alley by a monster? Did she think she was about to die while being eaten alive only to wake up to learn she'd become like the monster that had attacked her?" She heard the pain in her voice as she spat out those words and knew these people didn't deserve her anger, but they were part of Vernon and Steve's group ... pack ... whatever.

Orin jerked as if slapped. "Steve." He shook his

head. "Vernon didn't even talk to you first? You were just bitten?"

Paige's nails bit into her palms as she tried to calm the roiling emotions playing through her body. "I ... look, I'm sorry. I know it wasn't you, but from where I'm sitting, you're all part of them. I don't know where the line lies. A week ago, I was a lifeguard and a journalist. Today I can't seem to be around people without their scent making me nauseous." Her brow furrowed. "Speaking of which, how can I even be in a room with you lot and not feel overwhelmed?"

Georgette grunted. "We know how to be around each other without making each other work at blocking our senses. We've all learned how to rein in our emotional output, and we don't wear a lot of extra scents." She mumbled something low that Paige couldn't hear. "You don't need to apologize to us for being livid with all of us. We embody people ... monsters ... who betrayed you. You somehow found Tamsin and she can help you. There are few werewolves out there I would trust more to train a new wolf, especially a submissive wolf. She'll protect you and make sure you know what you need to know. But understand this, the four of us will do what we can to help you as well. We aren't dominant enough to challenge Vernon, but we can stand up to Steve when Vernon isn't around."

"If that's the case, then how come he's out there killing tourists and attacking people like me?" Fury whipped through her. Who were these people to make such claims while sitting in this room without following through with their bold statements?

Orin's eyes blazed. "I didn't know ... we didn't know he was killing tourists. That isn't something werewolves do. If they did, our secret wouldn't stay a secret. This is something that needs to be taken care of ... Vernon needs to take care of it, but I fear he won't. It's why there are so few of us in this room. Our pack, historically so strong, has fallen."

Maria sighed. "Orin's right. There was a time this wouldn't have happened. Steve is getting worse. I didn't know he had gone so feral. Vernon has been protecting Steve, keeping him under control. If Vernon can't control him, then, as a pack, we'll have to do something about it."

Connie turned to Orin. "Do you think Steve could've killed Elinore?"

Orin shook his head. "Why? She's not a wolf, not a threat, not anywhere around us. I can't see anything that would've triggered him. Vernon didn't lie when Tamsin questioned him. Vernon would've known and he's never been able to lie about his best friend. I agree it was probably the witches."

Everyone in the room seemed to relax. Maria

nodded. "That's good. I don't know about the witches. I've always stayed out of their business. It could've been natural causes; she and Clyde had been so much in love. Like Tamsin's parents, two hearts who couldn't survive apart. I trust Tamsin to get to the bottom of it."

Georgette leaned back. "Okay, let's concentrate on what's important." Her intense brown eyes focused on her. "Paige, can we help you with anything? History of the pack? Have you seen a wolf, or seen the shift? Can we help you train on senses or how your body works? We have a lot we can teach you. I'll need to get off to work soon. Maria and I have to leave in about a half hour, but Connie works nights and Orin works from home."

Maria checked her watch and cursed. Leaping up, she shrugged and gave a sheepish smile to Paige. "Sorry, gotta run and get ready. If we don't get in, the users will find ways to break down the computers and Georgette and I will have to reprogram everything." She headed out a back door.

Still not sure who to trust or what to think, Paige watched the motion of the people in the room. In the end, she knew any information was better than where she presently was. "If you could teach me how to be around regular humans without being dizzy and nauseous, that would be great. I can't work how I am now. Being fired isn't an option."

"Oh, are you hungry?" Connie perked up. "Being around people while you learn helps, and we can teach you over a meal. We could head out to get food. If it gets to be too much, we'll bring the food back here. I know some great places that shouldn't be too populated right now."

A grumbling from Paige's stomach answered the question for her.

CHAPTER 15 – WICKED WITCH OF THE WEST

Vernon followed Tamsin out to her car. Tamsin didn't want to share more words with the man, but she couldn't seem to shake the alpha.

"Look Tam ... er ... Tamsin ... I'm glad P's helping you."

Tamsin couldn't imagine Paige giving Vernon permission to shorten her name. "*Paige* seems like a good new wolf. You're going to have to get control over Steve. If the other packs learn you have a rogue within your pack, they're going to come down hard on you, you know that right?"

Vernon's face hardened. "I know what I'm doing. It was one day. It won't happen again. The tourist saw him shift and freaked out. He was about to call for help and out werewolves, and Steve decided to take care of it his way."

"If there wasn't any proof, the man would've been considered a nut. No reason to kill him."

"I know. Steve knows, but the man had a video on his phone. He'd caught Steve shifting to wolf."

"What an idiot. How did he let that happen? Did he do it in town?" Tamsin couldn't believe how imbecilic this whole scenario was. It took everything in her to not roll her eyes like her students.

Vernon sighed. "Not important. The thing is, Steve was still hyped up when he saw Paige writing the article. He recognized her from the beach. Paige may not've known us, but we kept tabs on the woman who'd written up the article on Clyde. Anyway, once Steve started, I got him to stop before he killed her. I figured having a journalist would be a great addition to the pack ... I saved her life!"

Tamsin sneered. *I should name the pounding in my head after this dolt.* Listening to Vernon stretched her patience farther than teaching basic grammar to high schoolers. *Maybe if I get him on a new topic my head won't explode.* "Witches. Where did you find the new black witches?"

The alpha's jaw dropped. "Are you going to go after them?"

"I'm going to speak with them. Have you ever thought about using your brain and not just your brawn?" She took a deep breath. Killing Vernon would be a bad idea ... right? "Tell me. Where can I find the black witches?"

Vernon bit his lower lip and stared at Tamsin for a few seconds, as if choosing his words. "Last I heard, they had a booth at the outside market. They sell candles and homemade soaps. You can look it up online."

Turning and sliding into her car, Tamsin shut her door and searched for the market on her phone. She put the address into the car's GPS and headed out. Once she found parking, she made her way through the booths.

One of the first booths sold canvas bags. She bought a couple. As long as she was there, may as well get some shopping done. She continued on her way through the market.

The idea of fish tacos for dinner appealed to her, so she searched for cabbage, onions, and tomatoes. As she took everything in, she found a man selling homemade brownies that smelled divine. A half dozen made it into one of her bags. Down at the end of the lane she finally saw a table with the sign: *Wax and Bubbles.*

As she made her way to the black witches, a booth selling homemade tortillas caught her eye. Smiling wide at her luck, she bought a bag, then finished her trek to her real goal of the day.

Behind the table stood a short woman with bright, frizzy red hair that flowed down her back, and vivid green eyes. As Tamsin approached, the proprietor's welcoming smile morphed into the expression of cornered prey. Eyes narrowed, her voice low, she snapped. "Leave, wolf. You know your kind isn't welcome here."

Tamsin whipped her head around, but no one was close enough to hear. "I need to speak to you and your ... superior, witch."

"We've told *your* superior that the time for talk is done. There's no friendship between witches and wolves. Leave, doggy, and stick with your own kind." Hate emanated from her tiny frame.

Leaning in, Tamsin growled out, "I'm here to determine if you and yours are connected to the death of my aunt. I came to talk. Your attitude leads me to believe the answer may be 'yes,' witch."

"You think I would care if a dog died? Fine. I'll

happily take credit for any death connected to you, mongrel." The witch lifted her chin and smirked.

Seething, Tamsin turned on her heel, and stalked away from the witch. Nothing she'd said was a lie. *That was easier than I thought. The damn witch claimed credit for my aunt's death. Next, I need to cool down and plan. I know witches are dangerous, but they will not survive this. I need to find their coven leader. Maybe Cinthia, Elinore's coven leader, knows.*

"Tamsin, I want you to meet Elinore. I know she smells different than you and me, but we've decided to get married. She's going to be your new aunt."

My nose tickled as I sniffed her, but she smiled at me.

"Hi, Tamsin. I'm a witch, and though witches and werewolves haven't always gotten along, your dad and my coven leader, Cinthia, have both given their blessing for our union. I hope that you'll also give us a chance."

I bit my lip and gaped at them. Why would they care what a seven year old thought?

"Come on, squirt. Elinore and I would like to take you out to ice cream. How does that sound?"

I couldn't argue that plan. "Sounds good, Uncle Clyde."

Elinore reached down to take my hand. Her skin was soft, but her grip was firm. "I'm hoping this is the start of a friendship not only between us, but between witches and werewolves."

"I would like that, too," I said, looking up at her. She had a nice smile.

Throwing the bags into the back of her rented SUV, Tamsin headed back to her aunt's place. One there, she changed her clothes, and went out for a run. She needed to stretch her legs and escape her frustrations before they overwhelmed her. She didn't have a pack to help her moderate her emotions, so exercise was her chosen outlet.

After an hour, she returned home, took a shower, and began sorting through her aunt's room, deciding what she'd send to a homeless center, and looking for Aunt Elinore's address book or a phone. Once a few boxes were filled, she ate some mac and cheese, and went back to searching. She needed to find Cinthia's number.

Not having any success, she moved to the couch and to think, wracking her brains to remember where she'd last seen her aunt's book. Where else would Elinore have kept her personal information, if not in her room? She needed to get her mind working, and the house wasn't helping. The pack house was only two miles away. She'd driven there in the morning, but movement seemed a better idea; she'd walk home later. If Paige didn't want to accompany her, maybe Connie or Orin could drive her back.

Halfway to the pack house she nearly came to a halt as a strange thought intruded. Why had Paige become a focus in her life? She could just do all of this by herself. It's how she'd operated since her parents had died. She didn't need anyone else in her life ... did she?

CHAPTER 16 – AND I POISON YOU

Paige sat at the table in the Middle Eastern restaurant. They'd finished eating an hour ago, but she hung around with Connie and Orin discussing the pack. Despite her better judgment, she liked the couple. She learned they were in their forties, and Connie had been a wolf for over half her life.

They had been part of Tamsin's dad's pack and kept hoping the pack would go back to the way it was under his leadership. "Vernon was young when he joined us, but not young enough. He has moments when I feel he could be a good leader, but they are few and far between. If Steve weren't part of the pack ... maybe. But he spends too much of his time focused on his friend." Orin sounded sad as he spoke about their current situation.

"If it doesn't get better, will you leave, or do what Tamsin did and become lone wolves?"

Connie shuddered. "I don't know how she does it. If I go more than a day or two without contact with someone else, I start to get twitchy. It's been years for her. She must be channeling a lot of anger into determination. She was a pack wolf through and through until the day she left."

Orin's smile softened. "How long have you known her?"

Paige tensed. "I don't, I mean ... no, that's what I mean. Vernon asked me to help her figure out what happened to Elinore. I just met her last night. I'm pretty sure she brought me over this morning to get rid of me. Find someone else to answer my questions and deal with the newbie wolf."

The other two just stared at each other for a moment. Then Connie shrugged. "Well, you're doing great. After the first few minutes, you seemed to figure it all out. Are you ready to return to the pack den? I need to get ready for work. If you want to head back to your place, I'm sure Orin can drive you ... or Vernon." Her brows came together as she looked at her husband. "Does he work tonight?"

Orin nodded. "He works, but the library won't be open, so Steve will be home."

Paige tensed. "Yeah, I'd rather be anywhere else."

"Then let's head back, grab the car, and I'll drive you home."

The walk felt good, stretching her muscles, and feeling the fresh breeze on her skin. When they got to the pack house, Paige said she'd wait outside as the two headed in, wanting to enjoy the nice weather. They agreed, and Connie left to get ready for work while Orin slipped into the house to get his keys.

Paige stretched, excited that she'd spent half the day around people, and learned how to filter out the extra information. It gave her a bit of a headache, but it was better than the alternative. Now she understood what Georgette meant about striving to make the others not work with extra scents.

Turning in place, Paige looked around the neighborhood. She realized she felt a pull towards the house behind her, something in her gut. If she closed her eyes, she could point ... not to the house, but to the three people in the house ... and the person to her left.

She opened her eyes and swiveled. She saw Steve approaching her. She sighed, wishing she'd gone inside, or hadn't come back here, or ... something. She just didn't want to talk to or face this man. Something about Steve rubbed her the wrong way. It wasn't that Steve was the wolf that had changed her—since then Steve had been nothing but nice—it was something more. An instinct told her to not trust the laid-back man.

"Paige, I'm so glad to see you. And you found the main house! That's excellent." Steve swung his arm around her shoulder. "Have you met the rest of the pack? Do you feel like part of the family, yet?"

Steve dragged Paige towards the front door. She resisted, still wanting to stay outside, but the other man continued to tug her.

Just as they reached the door, a voice came from down the block. "Paige! Just the person I was hoping to see."

Paige spun, disentangling herself with a shiver. "Tamsin? Did you walk here?"

The other wolf smirked, but her cheeks colored a bit. "I needed to work off a bit of my pent up ...

energy. It's only a couple of miles."

From behind her, Steve made a sound of confusion. "You walked the whole way? Don't you have a car?"

Tamsin's face flattened. "Steve. I see you're home. You can tell the others that I came and got Paige ... that is," she shifted her gaze to Paige and her brows rose in question, "if you want to come now. It's a nice walk."

"Yes! Absolutely." She'd answered before she'd even finished hearing the question. She just needed to get away from Steve. "But Orin ... he was going to drive me."

Tamsin gave a curt nod. "Steve, tell him on your way in, thanks!" She hooked her arm in Paige's and the two started their journey. They'd walked for a block before either of them said anything. Tamsin finally sighed. "Sorry if you had plans. You didn't have to come with me. I know I can be pushy. Were you and Steve planning something tonight?"

Paige shivered at the thought. "No. Steve just found me and was dragging me inside."

"So, I saved you. Good to know." Tamsin smirked, a twinkle in her eyes.

"Are we keeping score?"

"We are now."

Is she flirting with me? Why do I feel like I'm a few steps behind with this woman? I need to figure out how to keep up!

Paige groaned. "How about we just say you win, and when I poison you with dinner tonight, you'll see what playing with me gets you."

Tamsin laughed, throwing her head back and letting loose. It made Paige smile. Connie and Orin made it sound like Tamsin lived a quiet and possibly stressful life. It made her happy to help the dour woman to open up.

They walked for another block. Tamsin bumped Paige's shoulder with her own. "How did today go? Did you get along with the rest of the pack? Did they teach you anything?"

"Trying to get rid of me and all my questions already?"

"Yep." They took a few more steps. "I don't mind the questions. And if I'm honest with you ... and myself, I enjoyed your company last night. Well, you were a bit drunk, and that was cute. I'm curious what you'd be like less tipsy. But in a few weeks, I'll be leaving to return to Chicago. You'll need a more permanent network of people around to support you. I'm happy to help while I'm here, but you should know, once I leave Santa Cruz this time, I don't know if I'll be coming back again."

Hope and sadness warred within Paige. *When Tamsin leaves, where will that leave me?*

CHAPTER 17 – I KISSED A GIRL

They'd stopped at a store on the way back to Elinore's house and picked up some fresh fish. She knew spending time with Paige was a bad plan, but she loved the idea of connecting with someone ... it had been too long.

Paige gazed at everything littering the counter. "How about I sit and drink a beer and watch you cook. It's really ... um ... something. And then we'll have something edible." A blush colored her cheeks as she spoke of Tasmin cooking.

Tamsin slid up to stand next to her. "Maybe if you tell me what you were really going to say, I'll consider it."

Paige slowly shook her head. "I fear the answer may incriminate me."

"Ah, but you could also gain a meal cooked by me. She wrapped her arm around Paige's waist and brought her mouth to the woman's ear. "Your choice."

Paige froze. Her breathing came out ragged. "Embarrassment versus eating well. Such a messed-up choice." Paige leaned in to increase contact with Tamsin and then sighed. Tamsin understood that need to feel another wolf nearby. She wanted to imagine part of it was her, personally, but knew much of this was the wolf needing another wolf's touch.

"You'll eat well no matter what. I'll make sure what you touch tastes good." Paige let out a small whimper and Tamsin realized she was having fun. "You seem tense. Should I make you a margarita? It seems thematic, going with the tacos you'll be making for us."

She started to move away, but Paige shifted with her. "I'm still debating who I want to have cook. If it's you, then I can enjoy watching." Her body stiffened and she groaned. "I can't believe I just said that out loud. You're muddling my mind."

"You like watching me cook? Is that the only thing you like watching?"

Paige's eyes widened, then she bit her lower lip. "I don't know. We haven't spent enough time together for me to know. What else *can* you do?"

Tamsin debated her next action. She hadn't given in to touching anyone for this long in years. She'd given her aunt, and several months before, her uncle hugs, but she'd had her arm around Paige for a few minutes and it was degrading walls she'd had up for a reason. She wanted to pull the woman in for a kiss, but she knew that was a horrible idea.

With an effort, she stepped away. "I'll make us some margaritas. Now, as it seems watching someone cook is enjoyable, grab that cutting board, and start slicing the cabbage." She found the tequila, frozen strawberries, and the blender, and began blending them something to drink.

After making the margaritas, Tamsin sat on a stool and directed Paige through the recipe she knew so well. She had to agree with the other woman—watching Paige work was a treat. She could get used to this.

"Do I need to bread the fish? Because I think that really pushes my comfort zone." The counter was covered with bowls and plates of the different layers that would make up the taco. The last step would be frying the fish.

"You're doing great; just get that skillet, add some olive oil, once it's warmed up, and gently place the fish in, without dropping ... we don't want a splash. A minute or two per side."

"Are you sure that's it?"

"Well, you'll need to salt, pepper the fish, add lemon juice, but I thought I'd let you get the first steps done before piling on more."

"Why am I doing this? What do I get for doing all of this?"

Tamsin sipped her drink. "Besides confidence in the kitchen, and my charming personality? You should've bargained before you were almost done. I guess we can discuss compensation after dinner. I want to taste the food before I agree to anything."

Paige laughed. "That sounds fair."

It only took a few minutes for her to finish cooking the fish and compiling the tacos. They brought everything to the dining room. Tamsin filled their margarita glasses and sat across from Paige.

The first bite of taco tasted almost as good as the ones she made. Paige's eyes widened as she swallowed her first taste, looking amazed. Tamsin chuckled. "Look at you, making food that's not only edible, but yummy."

Paige slowly shook her head. "I can't believe I prepared this. Like, I did all the parts, too. It's ... I just can't believe it."

"I'll make a cook out of you yet."

"In two weeks?"

"Maybe. Just think, I'll have home-cooked meals every night while I'm here. I'm really not seeing a down side to this."

"Do you think the emergency room will give you a frequent-flier punch card for all the times you end up there if I'm cooking for you every night?"

Tamsin leaned back, crossing her hands behind her head. "I don't know; it sounds like it may be worth it to me. Watching you flow around the kitchen, me getting to direct your movements, and a meal in the end. We could come up with meal ideas together. Maybe find some tricky French meals with complicated preparation steps." She smiled wickedly.

Paige glared. "You're playing with me, aren't you? How about I sit and get drunk each night and watch *you* cook. I like this plan much better. And when you end up going back to Chicago, I'll pine away, missing your cooking."

Tamsin leaned forward and rubbed her eyes. "Okay, jokes aside, have we just agreed to have dinner together every night while I'm here?"

Paige gazed down at her plate and shrugged, then looked into Tamsin's eyes. "If you wouldn't mind.

I know you have things to do, but, I don't know, I feel drawn to you. Is it the wolf thing? Part of me wants to just blame it on that, but I know it's more than that. I've enjoyed our banter, along with the meals. And ... " She blushed. "You're beautiful. I know there's a limit on our time together, but I'd like to see what happens in that time." She ducked her head as if unsure of what Tamsin's reaction would be.

Tamsin knew the right thing to say was 'no.' As werewolves, they could easily get addicted to being in close contact, but she missed having a pack and people around her. What Paige asked for was something she craved more than she wanted to admit to anyone, especially herself. Someone around, small touches, talking about the day, not having to lie about who she was. She should say 'no.' It would be the smart thing to do. But there was something about Paige ... She smiled and said, "I'd like that, too."

They cleaned up the dinner mess together, then sat in the living room on the couch, legs touching. Paige leaned back. "So, big plans for tomorrow? Going to throw me to other wolves again?"

Tamsin let her head fall back, full and content. "I think the police will let me in to see my aunt's body. If not too many people have touched it, I may be able to pick up a scent. I need to find her address book or phone. Her old coven's contact information should be in there. That witch I met today all but confessed, but I'm emotional. I'd like to get Cinthia's take, and she's the only one left I know ... but I don't have her number or know where she lives. Then, in the afternoon, I have an appointment to meet with the lawyer."

Paige let her head roll to face Tamsin. She looked half asleep. "Who's your contact with the police?"

"An Officer Summers. He said he was busy until tomorrow morning."

Paige sat up straight. "Oh, he's great. He's always my contact when I'm writing a story. I could go down with you if you want. He may be more open since he knows me. We aren't quite friends, more like acquaintances."

Tamsin rocked her head back and forth, thinking. "You need to get down there anyway for your article. This way we can both get the information, and I can see you in action." She waggled one eyebrow.

Paige blushed but nodded. "Yeah, I do need to talk to him and get information for my article. If I could get the inside scoop that only the family receives, that would be even better."

Tamsin sighed. "Okay, but I get to edit how much goes out to the public."

"Absolutely, it's a date." A blush flashed onto Paige's face. "Um, or, well, you know what I mean. As for finding your aunt's stuff, or packing ... if you need help, just ask. I'm going to go back to work lifeguarding, but I have lots of downtime too. Just let me know how I can help."

After deciding to meet at eight so they could get breakfast at a coffee shop near the station, Tamsin walked Paige to the door. Before she left, Tamsin gave in to her desire and leaned down to kiss the other wolf. It was a quick kiss, but she felt the zing to her toes.

CHAPTER 18 – FIRST COFFEE ... AND SECOND COFFEE

Paige woke up early on Friday and stretched out in her bed. She thought about the meal she'd cooked the night before and couldn't stop smiling. She wasn't sure she could repeat what she'd done, but following Tamsin's directions had been fun, and the meal tasted fantastic. *I wonder if her version is better?* She almost drooled imagining Tamsin cooking the tacos and then trying them.

Groaning, she covered her face with her hands. If only she could go back to when their lips touched. Why had she frozen up? She wanted to kick herself. The motion had shocked her. She'd imagined the possibility all night, from the moment Tamsin had wrapped her arm around her before she'd started cooking. So, when it'd happened, she'd half-thought it was an illusion. She licked her lips and wondered if there was another kiss in their future.

She climbed from her bed and headed to the bathroom. Today she needed to look professional. After showering, she selected dark red slacks and a black and white patterned button-down shirt. She topped it all with a black vest, then went downstairs to brew coffee.

Pulling out her phone, she texted Tamsin. Want some coffee?

Her reply came quickly. You know we're going to a coffee house, right?

So, is that a yes or a no?

Yes, I want a coffee.

Paige smiled as she poured coffee into two travel mugs with a splash of milk. She gathered her things and the coffee, then headed out to meet Tamsin. She only had to wait a minute before Tamsin exited the house next door. The woman looked good. She wore dark wash jeans that almost appeared painted on, a light blue shirt, and a dark blue jacket. They met at the car, and Tamsin opened the door for her, grabbing one of the coffees as she headed around the vehicle.

The drive to the coffee shop was quick and the two focused on their coffee. Once Tamsin parked, they went in, placed their orders, and found seats. Paige sipped her caramel latte and waited for her sausage and egg breakfast sandwich. Tamsin sipped her large black coffee, with a splash of cream, and smirked. "You're having dessert for breakfast?"

"No, that's why I made coffee for the ride over. That was First Coffee. This is Second Coffee—of the dessert variety. Trust me, it'll make me sweeter. Don't you want me sweet today?"

Tamsin pulled her coffee away from her mouth as she shook with amusement, eyes dancing. "Oh, yes, I definitely want the sweet version. Wait, what have I been forced to suffer up 'til now?" Her eyes widened. "What are the benefits of this sweeter version?"

Leaning back, Paige narrowed her eyes. "You'll just have to figure that out, now, won't you?"

"Sounds fun."

One of the baristas brought their food, and Paige's stomach growled its approval. "I can't remember ever being this hungry. Will this tamp down or go away?"

Tamsin laughed. "Sure. We can pretend." She picked up her food and took a healthy bite. "Now, do you want to head into the police station together, or will that upset this officer you know? I could go in and talk to him, tell him I have a friend and then bring you in? What do you think will work best?"

"Honestly, Officer Summers probably will send me on my way. I'm not family. We can try to have us both go in, but he knows I'm a journalist, and more than that, friends are often told to wait while the family member is let in. If they were done with the investigation, it would be different."

Tamsin closed her eyes and drank her coffee. It looked more like she was thinking than savoring the nectar of the caffeine gods. After a few minutes, she placed her mug down and stared at Paige, then gazed at a painting on the wall next to the table as she finished her sandwich.

Paige got antsy, fidgeting with her napkin. "What are you thinking?"

"Probably nothing good. You said you can't come in because you aren't family. Well, what if we told him we're dating, or engaged. That way we can both go in together and get the information."

Paige shook her head, trying to make sense of the woman across from her. "Why? I don't get it."

Tamsin dropped her head into her hands and sighed. "Never mind. That was dumb. Forget I said anything."

Paige reached out and rubbed Tamsin's forearm. "No, wait. I don't think it was dumb. I'm just trying to figure out why you'd want me there, that's all."

Moving her hands to massage her temples, Tamsin kept looking down at the table. "You should probably stay away from me. You have a pack who can answer your questions and teach you what you need to learn. I'm bad news. I've been a lone wolf a long time, I could get attached ... so could you. But, I'm here to figure out what happened to my aunt and leave town."

"I know all that, it doesn't explain why you said what you said."

"It's just ... in the last two days ... I'm touch-starved, and I've really enjoyed your company. I'm just trying to find ways to prolong it. Like I said, you should probably run screaming in the other direction. I'm bad news. But, as to why I want you there, from what I can tell, you'll see and hear things I may not, you may even have questions to ask I wouldn't think of. But if she died of natural causes or it was the witches, I don't know what questions the police could answer."

Paige stopped rubbing and thought about everything Tamsin had said. She didn't want to run from this woman. She wanted to do the exact opposite, even if it were for only a week or two. They may be a few of the best weeks of her life. Why would she pass that up?

Paige slid her hand down Tamsin's arm and took hold of her hand. "I think being your partner for a couple of hours, or weeks, sounds delightful. I get being touch-starved; it isn't the same in humans, but we do have something similar. We just call it being lonely. If I can help you out in any way, then let me help. There's a good chance I won't be any help at all, except as someone to lend support, and if you're okay with that, then so am I."

Tamsin squeezed her hand back. After finishing their coffees, they headed out to the car parked outside of the coffee shop. The police station was across the street, half a block down. As they got to the car, Paige put her hand on Tamsin's back. "Hold on a minute."

Tamsin turned to face her. Paige took one more step into Tamsin's personal space. She'd been thinking about the kiss from the night before since it had happened, and she wanted to replace the memory with one in which she participated. She knew her timing was wrong, but after what Tamsin had said, she didn't care.

She gazed into Tamsin's eyes, which glinted a bit auburn, like her hair did in the sun. She slid her hands up into Tamsin's silky hair and pulled her down. Tamsin didn't resist. When their lips met, Paige closed her eyes, reveling in the sensation.

Tamsin's hands circled her waist, and her tongue traced along Paige's lips. With an inhale, Paige's mouth opened, and their kiss deepened. Their bodies moved closer, and Paige experienced a taste of heaven. Her hands slid down to feel Tamsin's strong shoulders. She moaned, feeling heat build throughout her body. Before she lost all her senses, she slowly pushed away, making a pained sound deep in her throat.

Her hands were still on Tamsin's shoulders, under the jacket, when she looked up into the smoldering eyes. Tamsin asked, her voice husky, "What was that for?"

Paige licked her lips and could still taste the other woman on them. "I needed a better memory than what we shared last night. I also thought it would help us act closer." She almost said, *and I've been wanting to do it, and only just now worked up the courage.* But wondered if Tamsin heard the words anyway.

Tamsin continued to hold their bodies together. She looked like she wanted to ask something. Paige tilted her head. "Something on your mind?"

"No, I've warned you to run, and this is what you did instead." Her hands dug into Paige's hips. Paige couldn't bring herself to push them further apart. "You're playing with fire, Paige Glass. I want ... it doesn't matter. You should get your story and work with Connie and Orin."

Paige's hands tingled where they lay on Tamsin's shoulders. "I'd rather use you while you're here."

Tamsin shut her eyes as if the words hurt her. She breathed audibly. "You don't know what you're asking. I warned you. But I *will* take whatever you give. I'm selfish. Stay with me tonight, after dinner. Don't go back home."

Paige's heart slammed in her chest. She couldn't believe what Tamsin asked. She wanted to scream 'yes!' but worried it was her proximity to the other woman. Taking a breath, she licked her lips, and saw Tamsin's focus shoot down to her mouth. She curled her lips in before she finally nodded. "Yeah, okay. Unless there's a reason not to before then, I'd love to."

Tamsin pulled her in tighter for a moment and growled low. "You're making a mistake, you should run, but thank you." She leaned down, gave Paige another quick kiss. Paige could feel Tamsin's craving for more contact before Tamsin stepped away. "Do you need anything from the car before we head in?"

"Yeah, my bag." Paige's voice sounded breathy. Walking around the car, she gulped in fresh air. The car beeped, letting her know it was open, and then she grabbed her stuff.

Once they were ready, Tamsin took her hand, and they approached the police station as a couple.

CHAPTER 19 - JUST THE FACTS, MA'AM

Tamsin's hand tingled. She'd spent years building up walls and teaching herself how to survive without the touch she craved. Something about Paige destroyed all her good intentions. And then the damn woman kissed her ... and what a kiss!

Maybe spending a week with Paige will fill a need I've had and then I can go back to Chicago balanced. Even to herself she sounded delusional.

They reached the corner of the block with the police department. Tamsin stopped Paige. She continued to stare ahead as she spoke. "Thank you for being here with me. I've been alone a long time and I know it isn't good for me, but it's what I had to do ... need to do. But ... I need to figure this out. An extra set of eyes and ears will be welcome."

Paige leaned into her. "It's what the pack family is for, right?"

Once inside the station, they found a person behind a plexiglass window. There was an opening they could speak through. Tamsin approached. "Hi, I'm here to speak with Officer Summers."

A haggard-looking woman in a brown business suit sat at a desk covered in pictures and knickknacks. She had long painted nails that clacked on her keyboard, and she smacked on gum. "Do you have an appointment, hun?"

She smiled at her. "I do, if you could tell him Tamsin Hath is here to see him."

The receptionist continued typing for a few more seconds before she looked up at her and her lips lifted on the sides, but it wasn't a smile. Grabbing her phone, she punched a few numbers. "There's a lady here to see you. A Ms. Tamsin Hath." She tilted her head and gazed at her. "Sounds good." Hanging up, she used her chin to point at some chairs by the wall. "Go have a seat and he'll be with you in a moment."

As soon as her message was given, she went back to work, Tamsin forgotten.

They headed to the seats she indicated and sat. She read the fliers around the room, most of them services offered with contact numbers, email addresses, and QR codes. She recognized several of them from similar signs hung on bulletin boards at the school where she taught in Chicago.

It didn't take long for a young officer, maybe mid-thirties, to come out. He wasn't very tall, just a few inches over five and a half feet, but looked fit. His brown hair looked practically buzzed off and his blue eyes pierced Tamsin. It didn't seem like he was the kind of man to miss much. His eyes narrowed a bit as they fell on Paige beside Tamsin, Tamsin's hand resting on Paige's thigh.

"You two came together? Paige, I thought we'd talk later. You know Ms. Hath?"

Paige looked at the officer and then her, uncertainty coloring her face. Enjoying the game, Tamsin lifted her hand to Paige's cheek, and pulled her in for a quick kiss. Then turned to the officer. "Yes, Paige and I know each other. Will that be a problem? I thought since we both wanted some of your time, we could do it together." She stood, grabbing Paige's hand and dragging her up at the same time.

Officer Summers's eyebrows rose and then he shrugged. "I thought you'd come in from Chicago,

Ms. Hath. I had no idea you knew anyone in town. I guess if you had family here, you've probably visited. If you don't mind having Paige hear sensitive information—she is a journalist—then it's fine with me."

The officer walked towards a locked door. He used his ID to gain access and then headed down a long hallway. "Let's start in a conference room, and then I'll take you down to the morgue."

There were already files waiting for them on the table. He and Paige sat on the far side, facing the door. Most of the papers in the file were written reports of the findings.

Elinore Hath was found dead in DeLaveaga Park at six in the morning on Saturday. She had been dead for at least eight hours and wild animals had apparently gnawed on her in that time. She had bite marks on her neck and her gut. The officer on the scene believes the bites to have come from dogs as she was found by a dog walker whose animals had gotten away from her. It is believed the dogs had begun sniffing and chewing on the body.

Preliminary findings determined there was poison in her system. The levels indicate a slow build-up over time. A full autopsy is requested.

Tamsin read the words over and over, trying to puzzle out the meaning behind them. Finally, she handed the page to Paige, and reached for the first image.

Before she could grab it, Officer Summers placed his hand over the folder, preventing her from seeing anything. "Now Ms. Hath, I've looked through these pictures, and they aren't for the faint of heart. I would highly suggest you just let us do our job and take a pass on this one. I know you're set on this plan of action, but I'd really like to sway you from it."

Tamsin locked eyes with the man. He may be human, but even they could feel the power of an alpha in the back of their mind. "Move your hand, Officer. I'll be fine."

With a pained sigh, he leaned back in his chair and shook his head. "Don't say I didn't warn you."

The first image showed her aunt's entire body. She lay on her back. Her neck was a bloody mess, as was her gut. She flipped to the next one, a close up of the neck. The third showed the gut. She studied each picture. To her, it looked like a werewolf attack, but she probably believed that because she wanted it to be Steve and Vernon, so she had more reason to hate them. Why would Aunt Elinore be poisoned if it were anyone but the witches? Spells can exhibit odd characteristics to norms, and poison was one of the tells.

Everything pointed to the witches. *Gah! I need to find Cinthia. This is awful. I've never had issues with them before, but this ... this is too much.*

"Why do you think it had been eight hours?" Paige's voice sounded calm and professional. When Tamsin darted a glance over, she had a pad and pen out, and her phone was sitting on the table, recording.

"It is hard to tell with poison, but we have a receipt from a restaurant she left at eight that night, and security footage of her heading to the park at just after nine thirty. We're estimating her death to be at about ten."

"Is there forensic evidence?"

"Not without the autopsy. With her gut opened to the air, internal temperatures couldn't be used."

"And this poison, do you have a type?"

"Again, not without the autopsy. We also don't have a timeline, amount in her blood, or many of the questions you're going to ask."

Paige smiled. "How many dogs? Does this walker often lose control over her charges? How long were they ... ah ... with Elinore, before the walker gathered them up again? Do the owners know?" Paige's voice lowered at that last one; she sounded a bit grossed out.

Officer Summers rubbed his temples. "Why do I like you again? Let me see. The woman—and no, I won't give you a name—had nine dogs with her. Four of them got away. Once she saw what they were doing, she had to secure the other five far enough away that they wouldn't get to the a ... to Ms. Hath. It took a bit of struggling to get them away. Once she did, and had all nine dogs secured, she dialed 911. As for the dogs' owners, I never asked."

Tamsin listened to the two of them talk, relieved Paige was with her. She just wanted to see the pictures. She hadn't planned on asking questions. As Officer Summers spoke, the scene unfolded, and Tamsin felt more and more convinced of what she thought had actually occurred.

CHAPTER 20 - PANTS NOW, DROOL LATER

Paige followed Tamsin and Officer Summers down to the morgue. As a journalist, she was used to asking questions, but she didn't often go to see the dead bodies. A thrill ran through her, thinking Tamsin needed her there for support, even though she'd half-wanted to be told she had to wait this part out.

Downstairs, a wall of windows facing the hallway showed a metal table with a body under a sheet and the medical examiner. Officer Summers stood at the door and turned to Tamsin. "Okay, I know you believe you want to do this, but I really think you should change your mind. You're what, a teacher? Do you understand what it's like to view a dead body?"

The muscles in Tamsin's shoulders tensed. "I understand you're trying to be a good man, Officer Summers, but please, let me see my aunt. I'm sure I know what I'm doing." There was a command in her voice. Paige was new to being a werewolf, but she felt the words deep in her soul ... *was that an alpha command?*

The officer grunted before stepping aside.

Tamsin approached her aunt's remains with measured steps. The medical examiner stood on the far side of the bed. He wore a white gown, a mask, and goggles. In his gloved hands was a file. "Ms. Hath, I assume. I've postponed this autopsy for too long. I know you feel you have something you need to figure out with your aunt, but this has only held up our investigation. Now that you're here, get your moment out of the way quickly, and let me do my job."

Tamsin stared at the man. Paige heard a low growl come from her but wasn't sure if the two officials could hear it. Paige walked up to Tamsin and wrapped her arms around the other woman's waist. "He doesn't understand. Let's focus on why you're here, love. They don't need to respect you, just give you the time you need."

A small sound escaped Tamsin as she leaned back into Paige. Her breathing slowed and then she straightened. "Please let me see the body."

The medical examiner pulled back the sheet, and Paige stepped back. Unlike Tamsin, she wasn't as comfortable around the mangled dead body. She'd seen a few when she'd written the reports, but always from afar.

Tamsin stepped up and leaned over the neck. Both the medical examiner and Officer Summers started to protest.

"Don't touch."

"Step back!"

"What are you about?"

Tamsin ignored them and continued to investigate, never quite making contact. "I'm not touching, I'm just looking at her wounds closely. I understand what it is to not contaminate a wound." She slowly moved down to Elinore's middle.

Officer Summers came over to Paige. "What is your girlfriend doing?"

"Searching."

His voice took on a droll tone. "I can see that. For what?"

How could Paige tell the officer that Tamsin was trying to find evidence of werewolf or witch tells?

She wasn't sure herself if she was looking for physical evidence or a smell. On a whim, Paige walked up to stand next to Tamsin, and took a slow breath through her nose. All she could smell was whatever they'd used to clean the body. The sight of muscle and bone started to turn her stomach, so she stepped back.

It didn't take long for Tamsin to finish examining her aunt's remains. "Thank you for giving me this time. I think that will do."

Officer Summers's eyes narrowed. "Did you get anything from your search?"

Tamsin gazed at the man, blank-faced. "If you could walk us out, Officer, we won't take up any more of your time."

The three walked out in a tense silence. Once outside the station, Tamsin took Paige's hand again, and they walked to the car. A warmth filled Paige at the small contact.

In the car, Paige repeated the question Officer Summers had asked in the morgue. "Did you find anything?"

Tamsin gave a small shake of her head. "They'd cleaned the body. Any scent markers left were washed away. I couldn't even get the scent of the dogs. I could barely smell Aunt Elinore. I could see the teeth marks in the wounds, but the smell coming from her was only the soap and antiseptic cleaner." She slammed her hand into the steering wheel. "Nothing. All of that and I've got nothing."

"No, you know that she died from poison. That means the witches, right?"

Her head dropped for a moment before snapping back up. "That's where I'll have to start. I'll search for my aunt's address book for an hour, then I'm off to the lawyer's office. Do you need to be anywhere today?"

Paige looked at Tamsin. She was taken aback again at the woman's beauty. "No plans. I can help you look, or pack. I can head home and give you your space. Just let me know what you want. I'm here for you."

Tamsin parked in her aunt's driveway, but continued to look at the windshield, hands on the wheel. She closed her eyes and licked her lips. "Care for some leftover mac and cheese?"

"Yeah, that sounds great."

Tamsin bobbed her head, then got out of the car. Paige followed Tamsin into the house. Once inside, Tamsin heated up two plates of food, and they sat in the dining room.

While they ate, Tamsin seemed distracted. She finally said, "I had hoped this all would've been easier. I feel ... I don't know, scattered. My mind is all over the place. Leaving Chicago, I knew it was

Vernon and Steve. I knew what I had to do. Now ... I'm lost." She took another bite and Paige saw how tightly she held herself. "I'm sorry. You should probably go. I'm going to be awful company." She rose and took both their empty plates to the kitchen.

When she returned, Paige stood in her path. Acting on instinct, she pulled Tamsin into a hug. The other woman's arms wrapped around her tightly, her nose leaning into Paige's neck and sniffing. Paige felt her muscles loosen.

Clasping her hands behind Tamsin's neck, she pulled back. "Is there something I can do to help you relax?"

Tamsin groaned. "I can think of several things, but are you sure about what you're offering?"

Paige lifted her head and gave Tamsin a kiss. Tamsin deepened it, pulling Paige in so their bodies pressed together. She untucked Paige's shirt and lightly ran her hand up her back. She pulled back. "I'd like to do this upstairs in my room. The couch is comfortable, but we're not kids anymore, and the bed's better."

Paige nodded, then followed Tamsin up the stairs. As she headed towards the bedroom, her heart pounded fast, matching the sounds of their feet as they clapped on the wood. She couldn't believe this was about to happen.

In Tamsin's room, the dominant wolf slowly

unbuttoned and removed first Paige's vest, and then her shirt. Shivers ran up and down Paige's body. Gazing into Tamsin's heat- filled eyes, she traced the strong lines of her face, marveling at her beauty.

Once her hand reached Tamsin's neck, she let it move lower and removed her jacket. Tamsin slipped out of her top and Paige gaped at how toned the other woman was. She let her fingers trace the lines of muscles defining her abs.

Tamsin smirked. "Pants now, drool later."

Moving robotically, Paige stripped off her pants and undies, focusing on Tamsin as she did the same. Then Tamsin traced Paige's face with the back of her hand. "There are a lot of things I'd like to do with you, but can we take a few moments to just lie together?"

Paige nodded and they climbed into the bed. Paige curled into Tamsin's side, placing her head on Tamsin's shoulder.

Tamsin rolled onto her side and signaled Paige to move so that they spooned with Tamsin's arms around her. Her warm hand began rubbing Paige's chest, playing with her nipples. After a bit, her hand slowly traveled lower. Heat blossomed in Paige's gut. Her body tensed as Tamsin's hand drifted even lower.

Then a finger dipped down to play with Paige's

clit and she jerked at the sensations zinging through her. She groaned and pushed into the magic fingers. Tamsin began stroking and circling the sensitive nub. Paige squirmed, rubbing up against Tamsin, moaning as the pleasure built.

Paige tried to roll onto her back, but Tamsin held her in place. "Let me play." Tamsin's voice flowed through her, low and dark.

After a shudder swept through her, Tamsin nipped behind her ear, and Paige rolled to her back. Reaching up, she pulled Tamsin down, demanding her mouth. Paige felt Tamsin's small chuckle vibrate through her as their tongues clashed. Paige let her hands explore, tracing the soft skin that covered the hard muscles of Tamsin's back. Her hand came back up to cup the perfect breasts, teasing the hard nubs of the other woman's nipples.

Paige started to buck as Tamsin took advantage of their position to penetrate deeper, sliding two fingers into her. Paige arched up with a groan, realizing she was about to break. Tamsin's hand moved faster until she exploded and saw stars.

Breathing hard, Paige opened her eyes to see Tamsin smiling. "That was a good start."

Paige licked her lips, feeling boneless. "My turn. On your back, woman."

"You think so?"

"Yes."

Tamsin smiled but rolled over. Paige pushed herself up, straddling the beautiful woman who'd entered her life. Leaning down she captured her mouth in a kiss.

Taking time to enjoy herself, Paige slowly kissed down to Tamsin's ear for a quick nibble. The other woman quivered beneath her, the movement its own turn-on. She scooted down, kissing along a full, lush breast, sucking the nipple into her mouth, scraping it with her teeth. Not wanting to let the other breast feel neglected, she fondled it to keep things even.

A low growl let her know the other woman enjoyed her exploration.

Paige kissed lower, until she got to Tamsin's clit. Using fingers and tongue, she licked, sucked, and played until the other woman orgasmed.

With her mouth on Tamsin, she didn't think she'd ever been happier.

CHAPTER 21 - BURIED ... IN PAPERWORK

A tension in Tamsin unwound. She pulled Paige up so her back stretched along Tamsin's front. A small sigh escaped her. "I really need to get to the lawyer, but we have a few minutes before I should jump in the shower ... are you okay?"

A sound that combined a purr and a hum came from the other woman, and she wiggled closer. "Do I get to shower with you?"

Tamsin's arms squeezed tighter at the thought. "Not this time. I said I needed to get ready for the lawyer's and go, not spend the day naked with you."

Paige looked over her shoulder to Tamsin. "But a naked day could be in our future?"

Every muscle in Tamsin's body tightened. "You'll be my death." She bent and nipped the other woman's shoulder, loving her taste. "I'm going to get up and shower. You are welcome to stay here, naked, giving me something to think about, or ... do you have plans for this afternoon?"

Pushing back, Paige rolled onto her back and reached up to cup Tamsin's face. "I'll shower after you, then dress. I can search for your aunt's address book, if you're okay with that, or start packing up some of her stuff. Or I can head home. Whatever you want. Again, I'm here for you."

Tamsin lowered her forehead to Paige's and let her body adjust to having someone to connect with. After a few breaths she groaned and pushed away. "I like the thought of you being here while I'm gone. I'll pick up food for dinner ... I may even cook."

Before she could dwell on the naked woman in her bed, she got up and headed to the bathroom. She took a quick shower, cleaning off and trying to bring her mind from bed-play to her upcoming meeting with the lawyers.

After drying off, she selected clothes in the bedroom and got dressed. Paige slid into the bathroom before she could get distracted. Tamsin put on the outfit she'd selected before, then found her way to her car.

The lawyer's office was in San Jose. The drive took forty-five minutes. When Tamsin reached the receptionist, the peppy woman smiled at her. She looked to be about twelve, with blonde hair pinned up on the sides and curls cascading down her back. She wore a fitted cream tank top, and a matching jacket hung on the chair behind her. "Can I help you?"

"I have a one o'clock appointment with Mr. Gold. My name is Tamsin Hath."

She gave a curt nod, then turned to her computer. A few clicks and she turned back, her smile bigger. "Very good." She stood. "If you'll follow me. Would you like coffee, tea, soda, or water?"

"Herbal tea, chamomile or peppermint would be perfect. No sweetener."

"Very good. I'll bring it to you. If you'll have a

seat in here, Mr. Gold will join you in a moment."

Tamsin walked into a small conference room with a circular cherrywood table with a high gloss. At the far end was a stack of legal pads, pens, and business cards. She sat at the seat facing the door, selected a pad and pen, and waited for her tea.

"Tamsin, I don't want you to end up alone." Aunt Elinore said, as she helped her pack her car.

"I won't. Just because I'm going off to live outside of a pack structure, doesn't mean I plan on being alone forever."

Aunt Elinore pulled her in for a hug. "I know, sweetheart. I just worry about you. You're twenty-four, and a strong wolf. I know letting Clyde take over the pack was a hard decision, and I love that you did it for him. I just don't want to give you up. You've been my girl for most of your life."

Tamsin could feel the tears threatening to spill. "I'm going to miss you, too. You've been a second mother to me, and I love you. I think this will be good for me. I can spread my wings, so to speak ... see what the world has to offer. Don't worry, I'll be back before you know it, annoying you and Uncle Clyde."

"You better!"

Tamsin blinked away tears as Mr. Gold joined her moments after the receptionist dropped off her tea. "Ms. Hath, please don't stand." He placed a stack of papers and files and sat at the table across from her. "First of all, I'd like to express my deepest condolences. Losing both your aunt and uncle in such a short amount of time couldn't be easy. Do you have other relatives?"

"No. They were the last of my family."

"Again, I'm sorry for your loss." He shuffled the papers. "Shall we get started in transferring executorship over to you? Your aunt has been working through your uncles end of life paperwork, it needs to be done within a year, but you'll need to finish Clyde's and work through Elinore's as well. I have a list of items that need to be completed for both of them."

Tamsin took the list and looked over it. "How much of this needs to be done locally?"

A sigh. "To be honest, you can do a lot of it remotely, outside of the funeral, but I'd like to take advantage of the time you *are* around."

They spent the next hour discussing everything

that needed to be done. Mr. Gold explained duties that Tamsin would need to do and what the lawyer could do. There were pieces that needed to go to the courts, and a document that Tamsin would need to carry to prove her standing in her uncle's and aunt's places.

While they'd spoken, Tamsin took notes. She had a list of things to do in the next week. She had to find Cinthia, pack up Elinore's house and put it on the market, find a bank and make an estate account, send letters to any creditors to send a final bill or she'd not pay. Life insurance, clubs, the list went on and on ... her head began to swim.

On her way home, she swung by a shop and picked up steak, potatoes, garlic, onions, asparagus, and a loaf of artisanal bread. She wanted a hardy dinner. She felt lighter than she had since before her parents had died and she owed it to a lovely lady who'd inserted herself into her life ... gods, was it really just a couple of days ago?

Chapter 22 - Wall Phone, and CDs, and Notebooks, Oh My!

After her shower, Paige ran home and changed into loose jeans and a t-shirt. When she moved in a few years earlier, she had stored her empty boxes in the basement. She grabbed the boxes, a roll of packing tape, and a fat, black marking pen.

Back at Tamsin's place, she started in the living room. There were large bookcases with books, knickknacks, and pictures. She searched through the tomes, trying to find an address book. She moved from there to the side tables, searching through the drawers. There was a buffet in the dining room with drawers. Opening each, she found silverware, napkins, table clothes, placemats, and—yes!—a junk drawer.

The junk drawer had screws, batteries, three small screwdrivers, gum, menus to local restaurants—she pulled those out and tossed them on the table—and the owner's manual to the lawn mower. *Huh, interesting.*

She moved to the kitchen and repeated her search. There was a drawer outside the pantry with similar detritus to the junk drawer in the dining room. This drawer was underneath a land-line phone. *Did she use this phone? What a throwback!* She lifted the receiver and heard a dial tone.

Shaking her head in amusement, she searched the second junk drawer. More menus—again, they ended up on the counter—owner's manuals to every small appliance in the kitchen, pencils, pens, a few small notepads ... *wait, that last one isn't a notepad.*

She dug deeper and pulled out a small leather-bound book with pressed flowers in two of the corners. She opened the book up and found names and addresses. With a sigh, her shoulders dropped. Success!

She moved to the living room and sat on the couch. She couldn't believe she actually found the book. After a minute of imagining her last time sitting on the couch with Elinore, she let the sadness flow through her. She felt like she lost the first person—people, if she included Clyde—who cared about her and her future. Even after seeing Elinore's body, she couldn't believe they were both gone. She'd hoped it was natural causes, but it was looking more and more like the witches had something to do with it. Anger boiled in her gut, thinking someone would want to hurt a person as nice as Elinore.

Using some of the meditative breathing she learned as a kid when she knew being angry would cost her another home, she calmed down and stood. *I'm going to start in a guest room.* There was a music system in the living room. She stuck in a CD of the Beatles, the only artist she recognized from Clyde and Elinore's selection ... CDs! Then headed up to begin.

She gathered the paraphernalia she'd brought and went to the first room. She left everything in the hallway.

Paige started with stripping the bed and putting the bedding into the washer. The washer was big, so she ran into Tamsin's room, found a clean set of bedding, then stripped the bed to add the used ones to the washer.

Then, she moved to the closets of the guest room, putting everything she found into boxes. She'd just begun the second room, when she heard the front door open. She finished with the bed, taking the bedding to the laundry room, rotating everything through the machines, then spun on her heel and headed for the stairs.

Paige found Tamsin in the kitchen. Relaxed from her success, and happy to see Tamsin making motions to cook, she spoke before she thought. "Hi, sexy." She slapped her hands over her mouth and felt her face warm.

Tamsin, who had been focused on something on the counter, paused, looked up, and smiled slowly. "Why, hello to you, too." Her eyes slowly moved down, then up Paige's body. "I think 'sexy' works just fine."

A shiver traveled the length of Paige's body as heat built in her core. She licked her lips and walked to a kitchen stool. "What do I have to do to earn watching you cook?" Her cheeks warmed more. "Or, I mean, how did your time with the lawyer go?"

Tamsin went back to cooking, a smile on her face. "There was a lot. Maybe you can help me figure it all out. I know people die every day, but, man alive, there's a lot to do."

"I'd be happy to help. I've never done it, but I'm good with sussing things out and organizing a lot of information." She saw a pile of papers and pulled the stack over. "Is this your list?"

Her only answer was a grunt. Reading over everything, her brows rose at the length of the list, but she thought it looked doable. As she reviewed Tamsin's notes, she stole peeks of the woman cooking, the only payment she'd need for any work the woman ever asked of her.

After a flurry of prep work, Tamsin asked, "How about you? How was your afternoon?"

"Oh, good. I organized one guest room and started on the second. Did you know your aunt had two junk drawers?"

"It's very Midwest of her, junk drawers. It's how we do things."

"Her landline also still works. I didn't know homes still had usable landlines. It's like an archaeological wonder."

With a chuckle, Tamsin lifted the phone attached to the wall and put the receiver to her ear. "That's amazing. Can you add that to my list? Kill the dinosaur."

"On it. But in the drawer under your dinosaur, I found this." She waved the leather-bound address book.

Tamsin gaped, looking at the book. Then she moved to standing across from Paige, leaned over and kissed her. "You are amazing, Paige Glass, and talk about burying the lead! Now, if you want to eat, let me focus."

It took her about a half hour to finish preparing the feast. Steak with garlic mashed potatoes, toasted bread, and steamed asparagus. Before they ate, Tamsin scrunched her nose. "Do you mind if I make a quick phone call?"

"Not at all. You'll be distracted if you don't."

She searched the address book until she found what she'd hoped to find. Pulling her phone from her pocket, she dialed. Paige could hear the message on the other end. "Hi, Cinthia, it's Tamsin, Elinore's niece. I don't know if you remember me, but I need to talk to you. If you could give me a call back, I'm staying at her place right now."

Message left, Tamsin poured a couple of glasses of red wine, and joined Paige at the table. "Next week, you'll make this meal, and I get to watch *you*."

Paige was about to cut into her steak when she snapped her gaze to the other woman. "I'm what now?"

"Do you need more incentive? I'm sure we can think of something in the next few days." Tamsin slowly took a bite of her mashed potatoes staring intently at Paige.

Swallowing, Paige focused on her own dinner, savoring each bite, trying not to think too hard about trying to recreate such perfection.

CHAPTER 23 - PUZZLE PIECES ...

Tamsin grabbed their dishes and headed to the kitchen. Paige followed. "You cooked, so I'll clean. And with everything you did, there are definitely dishes to wash this time."

Paige pushed her from the sink and began scrubbing a pot. Stepping up behind the smaller woman, Tamsin wrapped her arms around her. "Fine," she said, nuzzling her. "I'll just stand here and watch."

With a groan, Paige leaned back. "That isn't helping. Why don't you make us something to drink and let me clean? You're very distracting." Her voice came out low and thready and warmed Tamsin as well as any alcohol.

"Fine. If you insist." She slowly slid her hands over Paige's hips as she backed away. Over by the liquor cabinet, she watched the other woman's smooth movements as she cleaned the equipment not suited for the dishwasher.

Humming happily, Tamsin searched for something she could mix for a dessert drink. Kalua, Baileys, and some butterscotch schnapps ought to fit the bill. She debated blending them with vanilla ice cream. She found some in the freezer.

Drink made, she saw Paige had finished scouring the last skillet. She handed the beauty her glass of dessert and smiled. "As requested."

Paige sipped the ice cream concoction, and her eyes widened before a smile spread across her face. "Now *this* I'll happily learn how to make. You cook dinner, and I'll blend these each night. This is yummy."

Tamsin moved until she stood in front of Paige. She slid her hand to the other woman's taut ass and pulled her forward while appreciating Paige's body. "Why don't we retire and spend some time ...

playing." Paige smiled, sipping her drink. "Don't worry, you can bring that along and finish it."

Eyes wide, Paige licked her lips, and nodded.

The two headed up to Tamsin's room. "You put clean sheets on my bed?"

Paige blushed. "I was washing the bedding from the guest room. I thought you'd like the surprise."

"I do. It's lovely. But you know I didn't expect that, right? I don't expect you to clean up after us." Paige had cleaned up after dinner and had also done laundry. It was too much.

Paige shook her head. "No, it isn't like that. I just thought ... since I was packing up the room, I may as well take care of it. Really, I promise. I'll make a huge mess tonight and tomorrow, and then leave it for you to clean up."

"Okay," Tamsin laughed. "Deal." She drank the last bit of her ice cream drink and put the glass on the bedside table. "Care to join me in bed?"

Setting down her own glass, Paige came over to peel Tamsin's clothes off. Once her jacket and shirt lay on the floor, Tamsin pulled Paige's shirt off, then ran her fingers down the woman's curvaceous chest. Paige trembled as her own hands explored. Pleasure pulsed through her body with each stroke.

Tamsin leaned down until her lips grazed Paige's ear. She let her tongue slowly trace until it reached the lobe, then dragged it between her teeth. Paige grasped Tamsin's hips. A small moan vibrated through her chest.

Enjoying Paige's reactions, Tamsin sucked before slowly pulling away. She whispered huskily, "Do you know how beautiful you are? From the moment I saw you, I've wanted to take my time exploring your body."

Paige's breathing grew ragged. Tamsin's hands dropped to Paige's jeans, unzipping them. The sound of the zipper echoed loudly in the room. She rubbed down the side of Paige's hips, pushing her clothing off. Once the clothing was as low as she could reach, she maneuvered her partner to the bed, until Paige's legs struck the mattress, and she plopped down. Kneeling, Tamsin dragged the remainder of Paige's clothes to the floor.

With a slight push, Paige tipped back, landing on her back. Tamsin divested herself of her own clothing. She crawled over Paige, then lowered herself to whisper again into her ear. "I'm going to taste every inch of your body now. Are you going to stop me?"

The only answer she received was a small whimper. Paige's hands moved to trace over Tamsin's arms and into her hair.

Tamsin dragged her tongue down Paige's neck, nipping at where her neck and shoulders met.

Paige's fingers clutched her hair, and a small squeal escaped her as Tamsin's teeth left a tiny mark.

Tamsin let her tongue explore the ridges and curves around the other woman's shoulder. Under her, Paige slowly gyrated, making low mewling sounds as her head tilted back, allowing for easier access.

Tamsin moved lower, her own body buzzing with need, the contact building heat within her core. Her tongue traced down to Paige's nipples, taking time to investigate each. Taste, nibble, play. She sucked each one into her mouth, scraping them with her teeth. She used her hand to stimulate the other. Paige arched her back, increasing the pressure.

Swirling her tongue, Tamsin continued lower, until she got to the junction of Paige's legs, sucking in the small bundle of nerves as her fingers slowly circled the opening, then plunged inside. She lifted up her head. "Touch yourself, if that will make this better."

Tamsin groaned in satisfaction as Paige's hands moved to her own breasts to play. Tamsin found a rhythm, sliding her fingers in and out, licking and sucking. Beneath her, Paige moaned, and her breathing got choppy. A few high-pitched squeals of excitement were the only warning before Paige's whole body tensed and she screamed her pleasure.

Once the ecstatic cries subsided, Tamsin leaned

back on her knees, smiling down at Paige. "I was right, you are as tasty as you are pretty."

Paige threw her arm over her eyes, her chest rising and falling as if she'd just ran a race. "Give me a minute. Then ... your turn."

"It doesn't have to be you do to me whatever I do to you. I enjoyed myself. I'd be happy cuddling with you."

"What about what *I* want?"

Tamsin dropped down on top of Paige, her mouth lined up with the other woman's ear again. "What? Are you telling me you didn't enjoy yourself? Do I need to try harder? It has been a while. I *am* out of practice."

"God alive, Tamsin." She groaned. "More? You want to do more to me? I can barely move now."

Tamsin traced Paige's ear with her tongue again, reveling in the feel of the tightening of the body below her. She was so reactive. "Well, if you really want more, I could just play with you again. That was rather enjoyable, don't you think?"

Paige uttered a wordless moan. Her legs came up to encircle Tamsin and she kissed along Tamsin's neck.

"I'll take that as a yes. Because I have some toys ... I could strap something on and give you a good fuck if that's what you want."

A small groan escaped the beauty below her. "How about I fuck you, since you've already done me in."

Tamsin grabbed her toys, but before she could strap anything on, Paige put it on. "Choose your position. I'm going to enjoy this." She looked at the strap on. "Does this turn on? Will it vibrate? Pleasure for both of us? You really do have fancy toys."

Tamsin lay back and Paige lined the dildo up, slowly pushing it in. In a feat of dexterity, the woman placed a hand on Tamsin's lower belly and rotated her thumb in small circles against Tamsin's clit—a movement designed to drive Tamsin crazy. As the pleasure built, Paige rocked her hips, slowly moving in and out of her.

Tamsin growled. "I will bite you if you don't go faster!"

Paige leaned down and captured Tamsin's mouth in a kiss. Her hips moved faster, as did her thumb. Tamsin's body quivered with all the sensations. Heat built, with the warm tongue in her mouth exploring, the vibrator pumping in and out, the thumb ... good gods, that thumb. Her body was electrified from head to foot, and she forgot how to think.

"Cum for me, Tamsin. I want to hear you scream."

She did. Her body arched up, slamming the toy

deeper, getting more contact with the gorgeous woman above her, and her body sang.

Afterwards Paige cuddled into her, like two puzzle pieces meant to fit together.

CHAPTER 24 - MARRY ME!

Paige woke up curled into Tamsin. The other's woman's arm was wrapped around her, and Paige's head rested on the soft, but muscular chest. She spent a few moments enjoying the contrast of hard and soft of the stronger woman. Paige sighed in contentment.

Her mind froze. *Since when do I enjoy this much time with anyone else? My last relationship ended because I only wanted to see her on dates; I couldn't commit more time. And here I am, wanting to give any amount of time to Tamsin.*

Breathing in the other woman's scent, Paige relaxed. She thought about the day and ran through her "to-do" list. *I can't spend today with Tamsin; too much on my list. But I don't have to call work—* she looked at the clock—*for an hour.*

She kissed Tamsin's shoulder, reveling in her smooth skin. Finally, she moved lower. Tamsin had her way the night before, but Paige would get her way now. She was half-way to her target when Tamsin woke up. A smile on her face, Paige played in a way she hadn't the night before.

Paige sat on the side of the bed and stared at the clothes she wore yesterday. She shrugged and decided they were good enough. Reaching out to snatch her underwear, she felt a hand cup her bottom. She jerked up and almost fell onto the floor. Warmth filling her, she laughed and spun to face Tamsin. "You're incorrigible."

"You're the one flouncing around me naked."

Paige pointed to her clothes. "I'm trying to get dressed."

Tamsin raised an eyebrow. "What if that's not what I want?"

"If I don't go to work today, I'll get fired. Otherwise, I'd happily stay here all day with you ... with or without clothes. Now, should I head home for coffee, or is there the nectar of the gods here?"

"If you delay putting those on, I'll make you coffee and breakfast." Tamsin leered at her.

"Will I be late for work if I let you set the rules?"

Tamsin shifted from lying on the bed to sitting up. "Come here."

Knowing it was a bad idea, Paige stepped between Tamsin's legs. The other woman pulled her down for a morning kiss. Her hands glided down Paige's body as the embrace ended. "Yes, you'd be late, and losing your job isn't acceptable. I'll go start breakfast; you get dressed. Thank you for pushing back ... I need that sometimes." She grabbed pajama shorts and a tank top from a drawer as she left the room.

Paige slowly got dressed then pulled her phone from her pants pocket. She dialed the number for the lifeguard office. A gruff voice answered. "Paige, you're on schedule at eleven. I assume you're calling to tell me you're better."

She sighed. "I'll be there, then."

The line went dead. It was later than her shift normally started, giving her a bit of time to enjoy breakfast.

In the kitchen, she found a kettle of boiling

water. A French press was set up on the counter and Tamsin was filling it with coffee grounds. "Give me five minutes and the coffee will be ready. Is an omelet okay?"

Her mouth started to water. "Marry me."

Tamsin winked and continued to move around the kitchen. As sexy as it was to watch Tamsin cook on a normal day, her cooking in nothing but skimpy pajamas was almost too much. Paige had to bite back a groan, covering her face with her hands.

The clink of a mug on the counter next to her startled her from her thoughts. She looked up to see Tamsin's face inches away. "Everything okay?"

Paige cupped the coffee mug in her hands. "Yeah ... just tired."

A brow rose slowly. "That's it?" Tamsin leaned in and sniffed. "You smell good enough to lick again. You have to stop smelling so delicious."

She couldn't hold back the groan this time. "Me? *I* have to stop being sexy? I think you're missing the culprit here."

"After what you did to me this morning, I'm really sorry you have to go to work. We should focus on breakfast, then discuss you coming back tonight, if that's something you think you'll be interested in." She wiggled her eyebrows. "I think I'm addicted to you, though I'm pretty sure I can get it out of my system before heading back to Chicago."

Paige headed home after breakfast. She wasn't sure if hearing about Tamsin returning to Chicago made her happy or sad. She knew it should make her happy; they both went into this tryst with the agreement that this would be a short-term thing ... a long-term one-night stand.

She had about an hour before she had to drive to the beach. She started up her computer and began the article on Elinore. Though she knew she couldn't finish it, she figured she could get a good start.

When she arrived at the beach, she changed into her suit and a tank top. The day was warm, and the sun beat down. It was Saturday. The beach would be crowded.

She climbed up to her tower and a shudder ran through her body at the massive number of people populating the place. The scents and sounds assailed her, overwhelming her, as she sat. Bile rose in the back of her throat. Her hands shook. A keening sound hit her ears, and she realized it came from her.

A slow rocking brought her out of her paralysis.

She felt a vibration in her pocket. Pulling out her phone, she saw she'd missed three phone calls, all from Tamsin. A spike of worry shot through her. She tapped Tamsin's number and the other woman answered right away.

"Paige, are you okay?"

"I just left." *Is Tamsin becoming clingy? She didn't seem clingy ... well, we are spending a lot of time together, but this is too much. I'm at work, can't she give me a few hours?* "What's up?"

"I just wanted to check in. You're new to the family, and being a nice day, I imagine the beach is full. If it is, today could be hard for you. I know you've been doing better, but the more people, the harder it is to filter. If things are okay, then I'm sorry to bother you."

Paige drooped and her fears dissipated. "I was sitting here, frozen. What do I do?"

"Listen to me," Tamsin's voice flowed to her like a lifeline. "You've learned how to filter out the extra sounds and scents on a small scale. Close your eyes. Think about the lesson Connie and Orin taught you. Sink into the words and practices they gave you. Imagine expanding their words. Make them bigger. You're feeling overwhelmed because you see more people and your mind tells you that it must be harder with a larger crowd—but you're strong, Paige. It doesn't matter if it's one person, or a hundred. You can do this."

Tamsin's words lifted the weight she hadn't realized had settled on her chest, and suddenly she could breathe. She opened her eyes and decided she could do it. The families were just people at the beach. This was *her* job, and she'd been doing it for years. "Thank you, sexy one ... I'm good now."

"Yes, yes, you are. Let me know when you're free, and if I'm being too much, then that can be tomorrow or Monday. Though, I'd love to watch you making me shrimp fried rice for dinner." The line went dead before Paige could respond.

CHAPTER 25 - OFF LIMITS ... A SPELL

Tamsin put down her coffee and rubbed her head. When Paige hadn't answered her phone, she knew she must be overwhelmed. She'd debated going down to the beach and finding her. Her biggest worry had been Paige thinking of her as a stalker. She knew their connection was growing too strong, but in a week or two she'd leave, and that would be that. It may be difficult for a few days, but she'd survived through difficulty before.

Her phone rang again, and she answered, expecting it to be Paige. Maybe she had another question. Maybe she shouldn't have answered in terms of what Connie and Orin had told her; she could've been more direct. In the past, when she'd trained new wolves, they always whined that multiple approaches muddied the waters. Once they had one thing that worked, it was better to stick with that.

"Hello? Paige?"

"Oh! No, sorry to disappoint, it's Cinthia." She paused for a moment, then continued, her tone low and soft. "I'm so sorry to hear about Elinore. Is there anything I can do to help?"

Her voice stirred up many memories from the past. Tamsin fell into a seat and just sat for a moment, unable to speak.

"Tamsin? Did I drop you? This damn phone. Get a cell phone, everyone said. Landlines are a thing of the past, they all warned. I hate this thing." The last was mumbled.

"I'm still here, Cinthia. I'm sorry, I just ... yeah, I need help. Do you have time to come over today? I'd love to speak with you." Her voice sounded flat to her.

"Sure, I'm having lunch with some of the newer women from the coven; I guess some of Vernon's wolves are getting bold ... but that's another story. I can be over there between one and two."

"Thanks. I'll be here all day. I'm packing up her stuff."

"Oh, I'd like to look through it, see if anything would work for the coven. Could you hold off? The coven can help later."

She sighed. "Sure. I'll find something else to take up my time."

Tamsin got lost in a pile of old mail. She made a list of places she'd have to call on Monday to inform them they would no longer receive any of her aunt's money. A knock pulled her out of the paperwork.

The older woman standing at her door was just over average in height. Her long, black, wavy hair almost reached her waist. She wore a ankle skirt with lace and small mirrors with a white blouse. Her dark brown eyes gazed at her as if they could read her soul, which they probably could. Tamsin always felt Cinthia Olson knew more about people than they realized.

"Welcome, Cinthia. Enter in peace."

"Thank you, Tamsin. I enter in peace and hope for nothing but tranquility to you and yours." She bowed her head and entered.

"Tamsin, your Uncle Clyde has met a woman he's very serious about. We're going to her place for dinner."

Tamsin's face scrunched up. "Her place? Why not here? Shouldn't she meet the pack? She'll become a wolf one day, no?"

Dad shook his head. "No, dear. Elinore is a witch. I met her the other day and I really like her. I think you'll like her, too. We'll all be learning some new customs, but that's good for us. I think it'll make the pack stronger. I've always wanted the two groups to be better acquainted. This wasn't my plan, but you know Clyde; always stepping up!"

They headed into the living room. "Would you like some tea?"

"Yes, please."

Tamsin turned on the kettle and gathered some cookies and small cakes onto a plate. She found two mugs, placed them on the tray, along with a cup containing sugar, and filled a small carafe with milk. She brought everything to the coffee table. For herself, she selected a mint tea. Cinthia chose a black cherry brew.

Once they each had eaten a cookie, Cinthia sipped her tea, then set her mug down on the table. "How can I help you, dear?"

Tamsin took another sip of her tea before putting her own cup down. "I don't think Aunt Elinore died of natural causes."

"Neither do I."

Her mouth twitched in a grim smile. "The police report states that the body was found by a dog walker ... whose dogs found her. It's believed the dogs or other wild animals chewed on her over the eight plus hours she lay in the park."

Cinthia's head tilted. "You don't believe the story?"

"When I saw the body, I didn't see anything that disproved the story." She leaned forward, placing her elbows on her knees. "But the report also noted she'd been poisoned. Many witch spells present as poison to the human world."

Cinthia jerked as if slapped. "You think a witch did this to her?"

Palms together, Tamsin placed her hands up to her face. "When I spoke to Vernon, he was convinced it wasn't any of his wolves. He can't lie to me. When I spoke to some of the wolves who were my dad's trusted packmates, they agreed with me."

"So, it wasn't one of the wolves. That doesn't mean it was one of us." All the warmth had left Cinthia's voice.

Tamsin quickly put her hands out to the other woman, palms up. "I'm not pointing fingers at your coven. Vernon told me he'd heard of black witches in town. Have you heard of this?"

"Black witches? No, not at all, and if there were any in town for any amount of time, me and mine *would* know."

"Hmm." She took a sip of her tea. Tamsin didn't like the direction of the conversation. "I know I haven't lived here in years, but based on my memory, your coven and the pack got along. I ran into a witch a couple of nights ago and it was anything but cordial. I got the impression that if I didn't walk away, she'd turn me into a toad—or something less savory—on the spot. She all but told me she was the cause of Elinore's death." Her hands were trembling again as she recalled the confrontation. "Your ladies were never so brash and rude."

As Tamsin spoke, Cinthia seemed to relax. A genuine smile spread across her face when she finished. "This explains a lot. In the last few years, we've gained a few new coven members. One of them is a feisty woman named Fiona Michaels. She's young and full of spit and vinegar. She knows that the new pack alpha is to be avoided. She also has an uncanny ability to sense wolves; we aren't sure why."

"And she runs a candle and soap stand at the open market." Tamsin rubbed her head.

"She sure does. I'm convinced she'll be an amazing coven member one day, but for now she needs to be kept under almost constant observation.”

"So, there aren't any black witches in town?"

"No, no black witches."

"Could she have been poisoned? Maybe something in her food? Something not related to the wolves or the witches? I haven't been around. Is there something I'm not seeing?"

Cinthia sipped her tea. "The only people she spent time with were that neighbor girl and us. I met the neighbor ... Paige, have you met her? She's nice, but I don't know her. I guess it could've been her. We've had some witches leave the area, but I can't see any of them leaving this behind. We can do a search of her food, see if anything has poison in it."

Tamsin nodded. "If you know a way of finding the poison, maybe we can figure out who it was based on what was poisoned."

"If you can give me access to the basement, I can set a spell. I should be able to figure out if anything is poisoned in a couple of hours. If you aren't in the house, it will work better."

"I can go shopping; I need to get some ingredients for dinner. I'll take my time and walk to the grocery store. Before you leave, we should discuss the coven finding the things they want in the house."

"Sounds good."

She grabbed the bags from the open market on her way out the door. On the sidewalk, she texted Paige. My house is off limits for a few hours. If you're planning on coming over, let me know first. I'm not even allowed in.

She checked during her walk to the store, but no response came.

CHAPTER 26 - SPICY DISCOVERY

Paige changed from her work clothes into her jeans and t-shirt. She checked her cell phone's display. It was dead. She rubbed her temples. When was the last time she'd charged the damn thing?

In her car, she found a cable and plugged in her phone. It would take a few minutes for her phone to charge, so she turned her car towards home. She parked and trudged into her house. After a day at the beach, her body felt gritty with sand, and she wanted a shower and clean clothes. The empty rooms weighed on her, and the prospect of making it all the way to her room made her groan.

Paige shuffled across the living room, but the couch beckoned before she made it to the stairs. *I'll just sit for a few minutes, let my body decompress after everything I've been through. Blocking out all those people must've taken a larger toll than I thought.* Laying her head back on a cushion, her eyes fluttered shut.

Just gonna rest for a couple of minutes before changing for dinner...

A buzzing at her hip woke her up. Her neck hurt from the weird angle she'd nodded off in. *Why am I sleeping on the couch? Wasn't there something I was going to do?*

The buzzing happened again, and she pulled her phone out, answering it without looking at the display. "Hello?" Her voice groggy with sleep.

"Did I wake you up? It's six." Tamsin sounded somewhere between concerned and accusatorial.

"Yeah, sorry. I must've crashed when I got home."

"No worries, just wanted to make sure you were okay. We can do dinner another night. Go, sleep. You need to figure out this new world."

Paige sat up and shook out her head, taking stock of where she was and realizing she was losing her date for the night. *Not a date!* "Do you want company?"

There was a pause. "Only if you want to come over. Don't feel obligated."

As they spoke, Paige got up and headed for the door. She stepped out and saw Tamsin sitting on the middle stair of the steps outside her house. "What are you doing outside?"

Several bags sat next to her. Her eyes shot up and she closed her phone. Still talking into the phone, Paige snarled, "Did you just hang up on me?"

Tamsin laughed. "I guess I did. What are you going to do about it?"

She stalked over and stood between Tamsin's legs. She bent, put her hands on Tamsin's knees, and leaned until her mouth was at the other woman's ear. "Maybe I *will* cook you dinner, and then you'll end up in the emergency room. That will teach you to treat me right."

Tamsin's hands came up to capture Paige's face, and she found herself in a deep kiss. Her tongue explored the other woman's mouth as her hands slid down Tamsin's legs. She drew away long enough to purr, "Mmm, you're cheating."

"I guess you *have* met the next door neighbor, after all."

Paige leapt and would've fallen down the stairs if Tamsin didn't have a good hold on her hips. Looking up, Paige saw an older woman with long black hair and brown eyes smiling down at them from behind Tamsin. Obviously, she'd just come from the house. The scent of herbs and something Paige couldn't place tickled her nose. *I swear I've seen this woman here, visiting Elinore and Clyde. She must be one of their friends.* A wave of sadness washed through her thinking of her former friends.

"Cinthia, this is Paige Glass, newest member of Vernon's crew. Long story. We can get into it later. Paige, this is Cinthia Olson, coven leader."

Paige stilled under Tamsin's hands. A shiver raced down her body before she rolled her shoulders back and gave a small nod. "Hi, nice to meet you. Elinore would always say, 'I wish you peace and tranquility.'"

The petite woman smiled at her. "It is a pleasure to meet you, Paige, I hope nothing but peace and tranquility for you and yours as well." She dropped her gaze to the back of Tamsin's head. "If you're ready, we can go back in and check things out. The spell is running, and I think I've figured it out."

Tamsin unfolded herself from the step and grabbed the groceries. Inside the house, she started to put everything away. Cinthia sat down on one of the stools and watched, and Paige sat next to her.

When she finished, she turned to Cinthia. "Tell me what you found."

Cinthia stood and ambled into the kitchen. Paige sat and watched as the two worked in the kitchen, both Tamsin and Cinthia appeared to know their way around the room. Cinthia opened a cupboard and came out with a bottle. "This has poison in it."

Tamsin read the bottle. "Garlic salt. It looks fancy. Is this it, just the garlic salt?" She placed it on the counter and searched the cupboard. "There are a few other bottles in here."

She shook her head. "That's it; that's the only one. I checked them all, and that was the only one where the spell picked up any poison."

Paige felt like she'd been punched. "If I brought something from my house, would you be able to tell if it was poisoned?"

Cinthia's brows twitched down, but then she shrugged. "You have about fifteen minutes."

Paige jumped up and ran. She heard the others asking questions but didn't listen if it was between them or directed at her. She just headed for her house, down one set of steps and up another. She ran to her room and found the bag she'd brought back from her stay the previous weekend at the house that wasn't pack house but was one that Vernon and Steve owned.

As she searched, a mantra kept cycling through her mind: *fifteen minutes, fifteen minutes, fifteen minutes.* The contents of the bag lay strewn about the floor; it wasn't there. She tapped her forehead with three fingers. *Think, Paige, think! Kitchen? Could I have moved the damn bottle to the kitchen?*

She ran.

It didn't take long to find what she'd been looking for. She grabbed the jar and pelted out her door. A few steps down from her door, she circled back to make sure she remembered to secure it then skidded away. She dashed down the stairs and up Tamsin's and into the house. Breathing hard, she placed her findings on the counter. "Poison?" It was all she could get out as she tried to get her breathing under control.

Cinthia picked up the container and squinted. She turned it over, opened it, and even sniffed. Finally convinced, she placed it down and shook her head. "Yours looks clean. I can still see the markings of poison on Elinore's jar. It's the same brand, and I don't think it's anything you can get from around here. So, tell me, young lady, where did you get that bottle of garlic salt?"

Seated on a stool, Paige rested her head in the palm of her hand and waited for her system to slow down. A glass of water appeared, and she accepted it with a soft, "Thank you." Once she'd had about half the glass, she explained, "After Steve bit me, he felt guilty. He said his family markets that stuff. It's the best of the south, or so he claims. He gave me a bottle, telling me it'd change my world. I didn't have the heart to tell him I didn't cook, and it would be wasted on me."

Both Tamsin and Cinthia slowly turned to look at her. Tamsin raised herself to stand a bit taller. "Steve gave you that bottle?"

Paige nodded. "Yeah, why?"

Cinthia's hand shot out. "You can't challenge him tonight, it's too late. Wait until tomorrow. Get a good night's sleep. You know you'll be fighting both of them, so you need to be at your best."

A low growl came from Tamsin. "That ass killed her. He's going to die."

CHAPTER 27 - A NEW KIND OF BREAKTHROUGH

Tamsin couldn't focus on cooking or guiding Paige with dinner preparations. They ordered Middle Eastern food from one of the menus strewn about the kitchen. After they ate, she stood and engulfed Paige in a hug.

"I'm horrible company. I want to claw out of my skin and scream. I knew ... *I knew* it had to be Steve, and I let Vernon convince me otherwise. I should've asked Steve himself, but the man can lie." Her arms trembled with rage. "I won't be good company tonight and you have no reason to stay, but I really want you to stay."

Paige's arms tightened and her body relaxed as if she'd feared being kicked out. "Why? Why do you want me here? What good am I to you?"

Tamsin buried her nose in Paige's hair. After a moment, she rested her cheek on the woman's head. "You calm me. Make me feel centered. With you here, I may be able to sleep ... hold off on storming the castle until tomorrow." Her arms shook as she held Paige like a lifeline.

"I'll stay. A bit of snarling on your part isn't going to scare me off. Let's go lie down before you start breaking my bones."

After they'd gotten in bed, Paige's back to Tamsin, spooning into her, Tamsin's muscles finally began to loosen. "I never asked you about work; things just escalated so quickly, then I got all up in my head. How was it?"

With a groan, Paige rolled in Tamsin's arms so she could look up into her face. "Harder than usual. Your advice worked, but I've never loved being around so many people, and I couldn't help but hear what they were saying. How do you do it in a classroom?"

Tamsin stroked the side of Paige's face,

marveling at the woman. "You learn to adjust. It's been, what, a week for you? My first shift happened when I was eight. When you're born a wolf, it happens young. My senses were always sharper than the other kids', but after that, they got even better. My parents had warned me. Second grade was hard."

"Good thing you didn't bite anyone."

"Big assumption, ma'am." Tamsin smiled. She hadn't thought it was possible. "No one's really sure why, but a natural wolf can't turn a person into a werewolf until after puberty. Whatever it is that's in our makeup won't allow it. I don't know if a bitten kid could do it, though. No one has bitten someone that young."

"Who's done all this studying? Werewolves aren't out."

Tamsin kissed Paige's forehead, needing to express her feelings somehow and not having the right words. "There's a pack in Colorado. They have a private lab. They do legitimate work as well, but they have one division whose studies never go anywhere but to the packs."

"Can I ask you something ... maybe not. It's personal and maybe painful."

"Ask me anything." Tamsin stretched out so their bodies touched as much as they could.

A small sigh escaped Paige and she snuggled closer. "You said your parents didn't survive apart for very long. And now Clyde and Elinore. Is that common with werewolves?"

Tamsin walked up the path towards the pack den. There was a stillness in the air, and things didn't feel quite right. Her Uncle's car was parked on the street, and though he was always welcome—he was pack—she usually knew when he would come to visit.

Inside, everything felt worse. She closed her eyes but couldn't find her connection to Dad. She'd recently lost Mom and had tamped down on all pack connections. Feeling everything had been too much. She wanted a mourning time to grieve for her mother without feeling everyone else's feelings.

Opening everything wide, she couldn't find her dad. A whimper escaped her as she leaned against the wall by the front door, trembling. She heard soft voices coming from further inside the house but couldn't bring herself to move. Where was Dad?

Maria found her and wrapped her in a warm hug. "I'm sorry, Tam. He followed her. He left a note. He missed her and couldn't be without her. I'm so sorry."

Tamsin paused over Paige, her mind racing as she thought back over the different couples she knew. They didn't use the word 'mates' like she'd read in some of the silly romance novels, but she knew that packs had a connection, and she'd heard some of the adults talking about the connection they felt with their chosen. She wasn't sure what that was ... she figured it was another way of saying 'love.'

During one of their training sessions in Chicago, Nolan hadn't been his chipper self, apparently one of their older wolves had died. About two months later his wife passed away as well. They'd been old, and it hadn't occurred to Tamsin to think anything about it. She tried to think of an example of a werewolf alive today whose partner had died ... and couldn't.

"That's an interesting question. I don't know. I don't know all the packs and werewolves. I really only knew this pack and the one in Chicago. Packs are small. I'll put in a call this week, see what I can find out. Now, Ms. Journalist, thinking of too many things, we should get some sleep. Do you need to work tomorrow?"

"No, I'm on schedule Tuesday through Saturday

of next week, but I have the next two days off. The boss-man—the jerky one—scheduled me for today to make a point, then left me off the schedule just in case I really was sick."

"Lovely. Well, tomorrow won't be pretty. I won't be at my best. You may want to stay here."

A low growl came from deep in Paige's chest. She jerked and looked down at herself. "What the hell sound did I just make?"

Tamsin kissed her. "A very cute one. Let's sleep, we'll discuss tomorrow ... tomorrow."

CHAPTER 28 - FUR WILL FLY

While Tamsin showered, Paige ran home and packed a bag of clothes. Running through the shower, she packed her toiletries once she was clean. She gave up pretending she wouldn't be spending more nights with Tamsin; running home each morning to get clothes—her own 'walk of shame'—was ridiculous. Afterwards, she packed her computer and phone charger, and lugged her stuff back to Tamsin's.

As she entered Tamsin's place, the scent of

bacon wafted through the door, wrapping around her like a welcoming hug. The electronics bag landed on the couch, and she took her clothes and toiletries up to the bedroom. Paige returned to the kitchen. "Are you the perfect woman? Gah, bacon, coffee, eggs ... I'm in heaven."

After breakfast, they took the rented SUV to the pack house. The more Paige thought of the building, the more it filled her with sorrow. The building could probably house a dozen or more people, and from what she saw, only six people—wolves—lived there. It almost felt abandoned. Vernon and Steve did that ... or maybe just Steve. The man seemed nice at first, but the longer she knew him, the odder he became.

They parked and walked towards the door. Tamsin reached for the latch to walk in, but Paige placed her hand on Tamsin's arm. "Shouldn't we knock or ring the bell?"

"No, this is *your* home now. You don't live here, but you're part of the pack. You can come and go as you please."

Shock chilled her at those words. "I can come ... and ... this is *my* home? Like, I have a room here?"

"If you want. Didn't they tell you?"

"Those first few days they didn't tell me anything. Connie and Orin may have told me if they'd been aware I didn't know."

Tamsin grumbled. "The only reason Uncle

Clyde and Aunt Elinore didn't live here was because she was a witch. It's the only restriction. Otherwise, pack members tend to live in the pack house. Living among other wolves makes the wolf inside settle."

"What about you? You live on your own."

She sighed. "And I've been a lot more settled the last few days. I've made my peace with the decision to avoid alpha duels. I didn't want to fight my uncle, who always wanted the position. And I didn't want to take over in Chicago."

"What about now?"

Tamsin shrugged. "I've just grown accustomed to being on my own. It's like a constant pain you get used to."

Before Paige could ask anything else, Tamsin opened the door and led them in.

They didn't find anyone until they got to the kitchen and dining room area, where Georgette sat eating a bowl of cereal. She looked up from scrolling on her phone. "Tamsin, Paige; fancy the two of you here early on a Saturday morning."

A small smile played across Tamsin's face. "I need to talk with Steve, in the back."

Her eyes widened. "In the back. Does that mean?"

Tamsin's voice grew hard. "Yes, it *does* mean. Can you get him? You can bring his keeper too, if you want."

"Vernon's at work. There was a fire on the south side this morning."

Paige tapped her leg with a finger as Tamsin headed for the far door. All the nerves in her body crackled as she imagined how the next few minutes would play out.

Georgette pointed after Tamsin with her chin. "Go with her. I'll gather the rest. It shouldn't be long."

Her fingers turned into ice cubes, suddenly frozen in their motion, and her stomach churned. She followed the person whom she hadn't known a week ago, and now ... God, and now? She didn't want to think about now. She'd worry about her emotions when the woman returned to Chicago, and she could lick her wounds alone.

A door in the kitchen led to a huge private backyard. There was a thick wall surrounding the area, and Paige couldn't see any neighbor's homes. *Wolves live here and probably make a lot of noise. They've made this area private so no one will see the horror that's about to happen.*

Stepping up to Tamsin she pointed to the wall. "Noise blocking?"

Tamsin nodded. "We don't need anyone getting nervous as we play ... or fight. This is where we have our dominance battles. This is where Uncle Clyde died." Her eyes narrowed as she looked around, fists clenched. "And this is where Steve will die."

Dread washed through Paige. The chill from her

hands expanded to the rest of her body. "Die?"

Tamsin faced her. "You knew that's why we came here."

"In theory ... I just ... what if it isn't him?" Paige swallowed past a lump in her throat as tears gathered in her eyes. "What if it's you?"

She huffed. "Against Steve? No, not possible. He may get in some good licks, but he won't win. It'll be brutal. If you don't want to watch, I understand. You can leave. I won't think less of you. This is the side of werewolf society we warn people about. The side we try to avoid, but sometimes can't."

Paige reached up with icicle fingers to grasp Tamsin's face. The other werewolf flinched, then smiled as Paige pulled her down for a kiss. "I'm not leaving you. Do you hear me? Stop trying to convince me to run away. You're stuck with me. For as long as you're in Santa Cruz, I'm by your side."

A low grumble came from Tamsin. She rested her forehead against Paige's. "Thank you."

They pulled apart as the sound of people moving came from inside the house. "Paige, I want you to stand over by the table and chairs. This will get ugly but stay clear. Georgette and the others will be with you."

Heart aching, Paige moved to where Tamsin pointed.

A door opened and five people came out—everyone from the pack except Vernon. Steve's shoulders were hunched, his muscles tensed as he marched to Tamsin. Everyone else gathered by Paige.

"Tamsin, what is this about?" His hands clenched as he stopped mere inches from her.

"You killed Aunt Elinore." Her voice was low, calm, and in control. Paige couldn't fathom the power it would take to face the person who'd killed so many people important to her.

The two werewolves stood in the center of the backyard, facing each other. From where Paige and the others watched, they could see both of their expressions. Paige glanced between the two, her heart in her throat. Steve didn't look shocked or upset by the claim. His face contorted as a smile stretched across the lower half as if he'd heard the funniest joke ever. Then his eyes narrowed, calculating. A shiver racked Paige's body.

"And how do you figure that?"

A wave of power saturated the yard as Tamsin rolled her shoulders. "You put poison in that fancy garlic salt you share around."

The wolves around Paige gasped, everyone glancing at one another. *Apparently, Steve is known for the gift.*

Steven guffawed. "Who knew? You're actually clever. I knew you were athletic—and a pretty little thing—but I always thought you were kind of dumb.

Your family doted on you; families do that ... I hear. I remember, back when I first arrived, thinking you were an idiot and not worth the chase. Then again, you were a couple years my senior, and ran after the girls, so I knew you had a few screws loose."

"I have a few screws loose? This, coming from you? That's fantastic. But why go after my aunt?"

"I can think of several reasons to finish off your family. A nice bookend maybe? Finish what I started all those years ago."

Tamsin lunged, swinging her fist at Steve's jaw. The other man crumpled to the ground, blood splattering around him.

Maria stepped out. "You need to fight as wolves."

"What do you mean 'finish what you started'?" Tamsin roared.

Steve shrugged. "Your mom caught me burning a tourist I'd killed. I couldn't let that get out to the rest of the pack, now, could I?"

Maria sprang between them, arms out. "Shift, both of you."

Tamsin tore off her clothes, shifting as she went. Paige's mind barely comprehended what she saw. Within minutes, a huge red wolf with a black snout and black-tipped ears stood in the center of the yard. She was larger than average. Her head was lowered in Steve's direction.

It took Steve another minute to shift, but then Paige saw the monster from her nightmare. A large, dark gray, almost black beast. He was big, but not as huge as Tamsin.

Maria scooted back to the group.

Tamsin lunged, snapping at Steve and slammed her flank into the other wolf. Steve fell over, trying to latch onto Tamsin, but missed.

As Tamsin spun to get ahold of Steve's neck, Steve wiggled and snapped onto Tamsin's back leg, jaw clamping down.

Dancing back, unable to maneuver to Steve's neck, Tamsin tore into Steve's exposed behind.

Paige felt queasy as the wolves fought. She covered her mouth but couldn't turn away. Steve howled. On three legs, Tamsin spun and ripped out his throat.

Before she could retreat, a small gray wolf slammed into Tamsin's side like a sledgehammer, sending her flying across the yard.

Tamsin rolled until she was up on three paws. The new wolf—Paige thought she recognized Vernon—snarled and snapped.

Tamsin growled and Maria ran from the sideline to the center of the yard. "Stop it, both of you. Vernon, Steve admitted to killing-"

Vernon lunged at Tamsin, getting her front leg in his jaw and twisting until a bone cracked.

A whimper was the first sound Tamsin had made

since becoming a wolf. Tamsin caught Vernon's ear in her teeth and yanked. The other wolf released his hold and lunged for Tamsin's gut. He got one bite before Tamsin rolled, snapping at Vernon's leg, connecting with a jerk.

Maria ran in with Orin, and the two grabbed Vernon's back flank. "Stop, Vernon, and listen."

Vernon bit down on Tamsin's snout, blood flowing before the two pulled him away.

He turned to snap at them, then hesitated, a low growl escaping him.

Maria tried again. "Steve admitted to killing both Elinore and Janet. Tamsin's aunt *and* mom. What outcome did you expect?"

One more snarl, and Vernon pulled from them and stood, glowering at Tamsin, blood dripping from several injuries.

Tamsin made it to her feet, blood pouring from her snout and two leg wounds. Lips pulled away from her teeth as she growled.

Georgette came to stand between them. "You two can fight this out later." She turned to Paige. "Tamsin is going to shift back to human now. If you can stomach it, could you take her home? If you can manage to get her into a bath, that would be best. The shift will fix most of this–" she waved her hand in Tamsin's general direction—"up."

Trembling, Paige nodded. "I can do that. I'll fix her up and stay with her."
Georgette smiled. "Thank you."

CHAPTER 29 - WASH AWAY YOUR SINS

Tamsin leaned heavily on Paige as they walked up the steps to her house. Pain and guilt warred for center stage. Steve's death weighed heavily on her. There was no love lost there, but it was the first time she'd killed another werewolf. She'd seen dominance fights end like this before, but the death had never been at her hands, or teeth. She'd always wondered if it would be very different from killing the animals on hunt night ... it was different.

"Tamsin, my sweet, sweet, girl. You're a werewolf with a heart of gold. That doesn't mean you won't do things that hurt you inside." Her mom tapped her chest lightly.

"What do you mean, Mom?"

"We'll go hunting under the full moon, and if you feel the pull, you may hunt wild animals. When you hunt, you kill, love. It's part of the cycle of life."

I bit my lip, thinking about what I'd heard, and things Dad had told me. "What about ... do we ... um ... do werewolves hurt other werewolves?"

Mom wrapped her strong arms around me. "It doesn't happen every day, but it can happen. Learning to fight and defend yourself will be important. At the end of the day, sweet love, we want you to survive."

"So, I may have to hurt someone?"

Mom's face became sad. "I hope not. When you're a powerful wolf, it may happen. But not today. Today you'll just run and play."

A quiver ran down her body. She recalled the taste of fur and blood as she tore out Steve's throat.

Paige lowered her onto a chair in the dining room. "I'll go fill the tub."

Tamsin reached for her hand. "Use the bathroom down here, off the master bedroom. There's a tub in there, it's big ... big enough for two people. I can shower first, get the ... um ... get all the blood off first. You don't have to join me, though." Her voice was flat, numb, like most of her body.

Paige pulled her up and gave her a hug. A lightning strike of pain shot through her, but she refused to let the other woman know her tender touch brought anything but comfort. After Paige released her, she followed the other woman into the large modern bathroom with a slight limp. Though her broken bones had healed, she was still sore.

Her aunt and uncle had updated this room a few years back. The tile was gray with turquoise and white highlights. There was a huge multi-head shower that two people could easily fit in, and a jacuzzi tub. The counter held two sinks, and everything looked shiny and new. Tamsin would happily take this room with her, if she could.

After stripping her clothes off slowly, careful of her injuries, Tamsin stood under the warm jets of the shower and watched as Paige played with the faucet, finding a temperature she was happy with. Once the beautiful woman was satisfied, her warm gaze turned to Tamsin. A brow raised. "You'll need to do more than watch me. Soap is required to get clean."

Am I imagining her voice being low and husky or is there water in my ears from the shower? Shaking herself from her thoughts, Tamsin turned and reached for the shampoo.

She couldn't hold back the grunt as agony lanced across her side. The shift from wolf to human fixed her lung and most of her broken bones, but one of the ribs was still not healed. She rested against the shower wall for a minute as pain attacked her from the inside.

The ribs were the only reason Vernon had had a chance at beating her. The sneak attack snapped at least two of her ribs, with one puncturing her lung. Steve had broken her arm. She wasn't sure when her leg had broken. Most of her injuries were healed, but that one damn rib felt like a constant knife in her side.

Cool hands circled her waist. "Are you okay?"

She tried to breathe normally, but a hitch in her breath betrayed her. "My rib, it's broken."

The hands stopped moving. "Are you kidding me? Why are we here and not at a hospital? Anything else broken? Should you be standing?"

"I just need to get the blood off and to lie in the tub. I'll heal quickly enough, too quickly for the hospital. The other bones knit together already, and my lung. I just ... the blood."

Paige swore under her breath and grabbed the shampoo. "You had multiple broken bones? I thought I heard one of your legs break, but you were walking ... " She slapped Tamsin's hand as she reached for the shampoo again. "Stop moving. I take back everything I said before. You're an idiot. Dumb as a box of rocks. Why didn't you tell me you were in pain?"

"I let you help me, didn't I?"

"And *that's* supposed to tell me you have a broken rib? That you're injured?"

Tamsin shrugged, she thought it was obvious. "Yes?"

More grumbles as the other woman washed the blood first from her hair, then, grabbing the soap, from her body. Tamsin shut her eyes, basking in the sensation of the other woman taking care of her. She had no idea it would feel so good.

Lost in the world of sensations, it surprised her when the water stopped. "Come on, broken one; to the tub."

She opened her eyes and was happily surprised to see that Paige was naked. It was then she knew the pain was affecting her more than she realized. *Of course, she wouldn't come into the shower dressed ... you* are *acting like an imbecile!*

Paige helped her into the tub, then climbed in behind her, wrapping her body around Tamsin. "Does this hurt? Should I move away from you?"

"Please, don't leave me." Her head rested on Paige's chest. She fell asleep listening to the other woman's heartbeat.

CHAPTER 30 - IT TAKES TIME TO LEARN ONESELF

Paige had been cohabitating with Tamsin for a few days. They'd developed a routine. Paige worked at the beach from nine until three. It was only Wednesday, Paige's second day back at the beach, and though Tamsin said she was healed, Paige thought it best to keep her distance, just in case. *Can a werewolf heal a broken bone that fast?*

She rolled over and kissed Tamsin's shoulder. *I'm pretty sure Tamsin's asleep, I bet I can finish up my article before leaving for work.*

Twisting, she started to get out of bed, when Tamsin's arms wrapped around her. "How much time do we have?"

Paige slumped back down against her. "An hour or so."

"Hmm. Perfect. I've had you in this bed for days without ravishing you. I think I've shown quite a bit of restraint." Her mouth came down on the juncture of Paige's neck and shoulder and sucked. Then she bit down gently, dragging her teeth over Paige's now sensitive skin and she shivered.

Her hand traveled down Paige's body, stopping at her chest to investigate her breasts. Every muscle in Paige's body tensed, then she moaned, melting into Tamsin. Tamsin's hot breath and warm tongue moved to her other breast, taking time to lick and flick the sensitive tip.

Paige's hands roamed over Tamsin, her taut body covered in luscious softness. In reaction, Tamsin bit down hard enough to cause all thought to exit Paige.

With a snarl, her hot tongue lapped out. "This is my seduction, temptress. Behave." Then her tongue traced a warm path down Paige's body until she reached her next goal.

Arching up, Paige whimpered as Tamsin's mouth licked and her teeth scraped along her most sensitive area. Fingers slid in and found the rhythm that drove Paige crazy.

Paige's body gyrated against Tamsin, and she realized the moans and mewling sounds were her own. The world fractured around her, and stars filled her vision.

When she could breathe again, she curled into Tamsin, whose strong arms held her tight. As Paige lay there, she gazed into the distance, content. *Being with Tamsin feels like home.* Her time with Tamsin wasn't long, and a pain cut through her chest. *Is this love? Am I feeling loss before I lose her?* She tucked in tighter trying to banish those thoughts.

With a sigh, she pushed away. "Shower, clothes, coffee."

Tamsin kissed her forehead. "Shower, clothes, coffee, breakfast?"

"Stop spoiling me. I'm going to be a puddle of confused goo when you leave."

"So, is that a yes?"

Whimpering, Paige nodded. She sat up and headed to the bathroom.

Once she was dressed and ready for work, she found Tamsin in the kitchen in her skimpy pajamas. Her movements flowed like water over rocks in a stream. Paige sat on a stool and tried not to drool ... *over the food, that's right, the food.*

A mug of coffee appeared in front of her like magic. She sighed. "I'm in love."

Tamsin snorted. "I would be honored, but I'm

pretty sure you're talking to the coffee."

"Hmm." Paige responded noncommittally.

A few minutes later, Tamsin set a plate with two slices of buttery bread, toasted to perfection with fried eggs cooked in the center in front of her. She couldn't even describe how good it looked and smelled. She took a bite and moaned.

A blush heated her cheeks. "Can you just pretend you didn't hear me make any of the sounds I've made since ... well, probably since I woke up?"

"Gods, no! The sounds you make are one of my favorite things about you. They're fantastic. It's a game: what can I do to get you to make new noises?"

Paige's head dropped to her forearm. "I want to believe you're joking with me, but I'm guessing you're not."

A laugh was her only answer.

When they'd finished eating, Paige gathered their plates and took them into the kitchen. Tamsin's phone rang while she loaded the dishwasher.

Tamsin sauntered into the master bedroom for privacy. When she came back, her face was drawn, mouth hard, eyes flat. "That was Officer Summers. He told me that the poison found in Aunt Elinor's system is known to accumulate and kill over the long term. It has no taste or scent. I'm going to bring the garlic salt to the station for them to test."

"Do you want me to call in sick?"

Tamsin came up and wrapped her arms around Paige. "No, you go to work. I won't be alone. Cinthia will be around to help me pack later today. You'll be home by three thirty to four. I'll survive that long."

Paige clasped her hands behind Tamsin's neck. "If you're sure. You know ... I hope you know ... I mean ... I'll make you a priority. You're important to me."

Tamsin rested her chin on Paige's head. "Thank you. You're important to me, too, which is why I don't want you to get fired. There's a bag lunch in the fridge for you, so you remember who's feeding you and don't get distracted by all the hot women in skimpy bikinis on the beach."

Laughing, Paige gave her a hug, then grabbed the lunch before heading out to her car. The idea that she'd find another woman ... another person ... in any way better than Tamsin, just didn't compute.

Chapter 31 - The Werewolf, The Witch, and The Wardrobe

Tamsin went up to her room to shower and dress. She thought about Paige. The connection between the two of them. *Do Paige or Vernon realize she's connected to me, and not Vernon's pack?* She'd known for sure when Paige had gone back to work. They'd have to do something about that before she left, but for now, having a pack, even a two person pack, soothed her.

Today's goal was to pack up the master bedroom. She wanted to sort through the papers and knickknacks in that room, and maybe the living room. She would keep a few as mementos of her relatives. Some would go to charity. Finally, she'd gotten around to packing. Two days of making phone calls, being put on hold, and talking to entry-level employees who didn't want to be taking her call in the first place. It had been hell.

She'd finished filling a box with items from Clyde's bedside table, when the doorbell rang. Slumping, she took a moment to grumble, before she stood, then made her way to the door. Everyone from Vernon's pack, save Vernon, stood waiting on the front stoop. Though she was happy to see her old pack, friends ... family, she didn't have time to socialize. She had a plan for the day, and meeting with these four people hadn't been part of it.

"Please, come in, make yourself at home. Would anyone like coffee or tea?"

Georgette sighed. "Coffee would be lovely."

"Coffee for me and Connie as well, with milk and sugar." Orin smiled as he made his way to the living room.

Maria shook her head. "Tea, please."

It took a few minutes to heat up the water. She poured hot water over fresh ground beans, then filled a small pot and placed it on a tray with everything else and brought it into the living room so everyone could serve themselves. More coffee would be needed, so she started heating another kettle of water.

She sat in a chair and faced the others. Georgette sipped her coffee and sighed. "I assume you know by now that Paige isn't part of our pack."

Tamsin grunted and sipped her coffee. It figured Georgette would know; she was always the clever one.

Georgette tilted her head. "Are you forming a pack?"

Tamsin's face fell. "No. I didn't mean to collect her; I'm not really sure how it happened. I was hoping no one would notice. We can get it all sorted out before I leave."

Maria's smile stretched across her face. "You like having someone connected to you, don't you? It's been too long—you living alone."

Connie watched her as she tried to keep a blank face. "I've lived without a pack, but only when I wasn't a werewolf. It's a lonely life. Since I was bitten, I can't imagine doing what you do. Orin and I went on vacation a couple of years ago, and even with just two of us it grew difficult not having others around."

Tamsin waited. Connie wasn't sharing anything she didn't already know, didn't live.

Orin huffed. "Vernon isn't a good alpha. He frustrated half the pack. It drove them away. He's alienated the witches. The only reason we stayed is our family and jobs. In the few days since Steve died, he's gotten worse. As hard as it is to believe, I think Steve calmed him down."

Tamsin leaned forward. "Were they a couple?"

All four of her guests looked off into space, thinking. Maria spoke first. "No, they both dated women, but they were connected like they were in a relationship. They did everything together."

Watching the four wolves in her living room, Tamsin wondered if there was something between the two men the others didn't know about. She thought back to what Paige had asked, about whether two wolves could be connected to the point that they couldn't live without each other. Could Vernon and Steve be like that?

I wonder what that kind of connection feels like. Tamsin jerked in her seat, as it hit her. *Do I know?*

"Tamsin, I can't live without your mother. My heart breaks every night when I go to bed and she isn't there and every morning when I wake alone. I know it isn't fair to you, but I don't think I can go

on any longer without her. I love you, dear, but I must go find her."

Ever observant, Georgette's eyes narrowed. "Are you okay?"

"Yeah, I'm fine. Why did the four of you come today?"

Orin placed his mug on the tray. "We want you to take over as alpha."

It felt like she'd been punched in the gut. "What?"

Orin continued. "The last time we had a truly great alpha was when your father led us. Clyde was good, but he didn't have what your dad had. What you have. We need you. Please, come back to the pack. Rebuild your family's legacy."

A stirring in her gut called to her, but she couldn't. "I can't. I have a life in Chicago, a job, and responsibilities. I can't just not return."

Maria slouched. "Just think about it. We know you need to finish out the school year, but we need you too."

They talked for a bit longer, and then they left. Maria and Georgette had to work.

Tamsin headed back to the master bedroom to

continue packing. She finished Clyde's side of the room and stacked the boxes by the front door. She was about to return to the bedroom when the doorbell rang again.

She muttered a few choice words as she stalked to the front and swung open the door. Cinthia stood beside the spit-fire woman from the open market, Fiona. A third woman stood behind them. A bit taller than Cinthia or Fiona, with brown hair and eyes. All three of them looked ready to work.

Tamsin stepped back and waved her arm in a grandiose sweep. "Ladies."

Cinthia strode into the kitchen. "I'm going to make tea. I brought some pastries, as well."

Everyone gathered around the island. Tamsin fetched mugs and tea bags while Cinthia got the kettle going.

Once everyone had tea and a few fruit pastries, they spread throughout the house. Tamsin returned to the bedroom with Cinthia. The other two headed to pack the dining room.

Cinthia went to the closet while Tamsin continued with the drawers. Tamsin needed to talk after her previous guests. "The pack wants me to relocate here."

"If you did, would you want to live here?"

"What?" Tamsin shot a look at the witch. "No,

of course not. This house has never been my home. The others want me to take over the pack. If I came back, I'd live with them in the pack house. Why are we even talking like this? I'm not coming back; my home is Chicago."

"Why?" Her voice was muffled from all the clothes in the closet. "Do you mind if I keep some of these?" She waved a few of the dresses out the closet door.

"No, I don't mind. And I'm not coming back here because I have a job there."

"But you have a life here. I'm sure you could find a job here, too. You seem to enjoy your time with Paige, and you have a pack that needs you. And Tamsin, you need a pack. You've lived without other wolves for too long. I can tell you're more stable even after just a few days with Paige."

"What?" She stopped packing this time and gaped at the witch.

"You know I can see more of you than what you present. That woman is good for you. I've never seen you so level. But it's just my opinion. I could be imagining things."

Tamsin narrowed her eyes. "Yeah, I think you are. I'll be fine back in Chicago." She went back to packing.

While sorting through the items in each drawer,

she found an envelope with both her and Cinthia's name on it. She gazed at the envelope and her hand began to tremble.

"Cinthia." Her voice shook. The other woman came to sit next to her on the bed.

She opened the envelope and started to read.

Dear Tamsin and Cinthia-

The last six months without Clyde has shown me that life without him is miserable. I love you both, as family and friend, and hope you understand. A piece of my heart has left me, and Tamsin, like your father did years ago, I need to go find that missing piece.

I have tried to live without Clyde, and for a while I believe it was a possibility. However, in the end, I miss my heart too much.

Tamsin, know that I am truly sorry for not talking to you before I made this decision. I am leaving you alone in the world. I hope you find love. You need to be with other people, others of your kind. Being alone will kill you as surely as the seasoning I've been adding to my meals.

Cinthia, you have been a sister to me for so many years. I've tried to tell you the truth of loving a man like Clyde. I don't know that anyone can understand the depth of that love. Maybe someone can survive this soul-crushing sadness, but I am not that strong. Forgive me for leaving you like this.

Much love to you both,
Elinore Hath

CHAPTER 32 - THE OFFER

Paige sat with Tamsin in the living room, cuddled together on the couch. Her article was scheduled to drop today. She'd finished it last Friday, two days after Tamsin found the note from Elinore.

After finding the note, Tamsin and Cinthia decided to bring it to the police. Elinore had been careful; nothing in the note mentioned anything about werewolves or witches.

Officer Summers told them the investigation was closed after receiving the spice bottle and note. He thanked them for the information they diligently reported.

Just about everything from the house was packed up. Paige gazed at the mostly empty house and felt a hollow sorrow well up inside her, seeking an exit. She was going to lose Tamsin this week, and it hurt ... physically hurt. "When are you putting the house on the market?"

Tamsin, who sat behind her, tightened her hold. "Trying to get rid of me?"

"Totally." Her voice came out so low, she barely heard it herself. She had to snap out of it. She'd promised Tamsin she wouldn't be that person.

"Paige, what's wro—" Her phone buzzed. "Hold that thought." She slipped the phone out and answered it. "Cinthia. Can I help you?"

Since becoming a werewolf, Paige had learned how to tamp down on her werewolf "superpowers." As she understood it, they would intensify once she actually became a wolf. The first full moon was the following week. She could shift whenever she wanted after her first time, but the first shift was bound to the moon.

The one sense with which she had a mixed love-hate relationship, was hearing. At times, being able to hear everything drove her crazy. When she could hear both sides of a conversation, it made things easier.

"Morning, Tamsin. I've been talking to the other members of the coven. We had a full circle meeting on Sunday. We've come to a decision."

"Oh? Anything I would be interested in?"

"Well, you see, your aunt's house is in a perfect location, and her basement is a great place for spells. What I'm saying is, we'd like to purchase the house from you, if you'd be okay with that."

Paige felt Tamsin's muscles tense under her. "You want to buy the house? For a fair value price?"

"Of course. The coven has a certain amount of funds. We'll hire an inspector and get a quote."

Tamsin squeezed Paige. "Then yes, that sounds great!"

The two spoke for a few more minutes before Tamsin signed off. "Did you hear that? The last big item is checked off my list. Once the paperwork is done, I can arrange my return to Chicago."

A knife in my heart wouldn't hurt this much. "I could come with you." The words tumbled from her mouth before she realized what she'd said. She slapped her hands over her mouth, wanting to stuff the words back in. It wasn't that she didn't like the idea, she just feared what Tamsin would think.

Tamsin tensed. "You could what?"

She slumped. "I'm sorry. I've been trying to keep

everything light, like you wanted, but I can't help it. You're like a rascal who's snuck in and stolen my heart. I can't imagine not waking up with you, not having you around to banter with. I know ... I'm being too much."

Paige prepared herself to run when the verbal smackdown came. She hadn't said everything, but she'd said as much as she could without tearing out her heart.

Much to her surprise, Tamsin's arms continued to hold her tight. "I don't know who in this scenario is the rascal, or who stole who's heart. Don't offer something you can't follow through with. I've been thinking about ways to steal you away, but there isn't an ocean in Chicago."

Covering her eyes, Paige decided it was time. In for a penny and all that. "I love you, Tamsin. I can write articles anywhere. I only work at the beach for money to pay for that expensive house I own. If I had a roommate, I probably could live off one income."

"And you never need to go into the office. But you always have to go on location."

"I can probably get another journalism job in Chicago. And if not a writing job, something. I'm versatile ... outside of cooking."

Tamsin laughed. She rolled over, pulling Paige

on top of her so they lay face to face. "I love you too, Paige Glass. I never thought I'd find someone I wanted to wake up with every day, someone to challenge me, but here you are, and I don't want to let you go. I can't believe you're making this offer."

They spent the rest of the day celebrating.

CHAPTER 33 - THE GAUNTLET IS DROPPED

"Hurry up. The open house starts in twenty minutes."

Paige glared at her. "My house is next door, the realtor is already there, and everything is set. It isn't like we even have to *be* there for the open house."

Most of Paige's belongings were boxed up in storage pods waiting for a final location. Tamsin's small, third-floor walk-up apartment in Chicago was too small. They'd need to find something a bit bigger. Paige assured her she could survive with her clothes and computer for the time being. A life in foster care taught her how to live lightly.

Paige skipped down the stairs in a fitted green dress that matched her eyes and a black shawl slung over her shoulders. Her reddish blond curls hair looked tousled. She could be on the cover of a magazine. Naughty thoughts and ideas flitted through Tamsin's mind of what she'd do to and with Paige ... later, when she could unwrap such a lovely gift in private.

She quickly turned and sipped her coffee. They had things to do today, and indulging her thoughts were not going to get them out of the house.

Paige gave her a hug from behind. "Any coffee for me?" She yawned and stepped away to stretch.

Tamsin reached for the second mug she'd prepared. "If I want you to be functional today, then yes."

With a grunt, Paige sat down at the table. "So, we'll stop in at the open house, which we really don't need to do. Then what? Why am I all gussied up?"

"I want to take you out on a date. We could drive up to San Francisco for the day. Have a nice dinner. Get a hotel for the night."

A smile blossomed on Paige's face. "It hadn't even occurred to me. We haven't been on a date. Well, I think you should ask me first, not just assume."

Warmth spread through Tamsin's body. She loved this person who teased and challenged her. *Love. Who thought I'd ever feel that way about anyone?* She pulled Paige to her feet, wrapping her arms around the woman's waist, and resting her hands on her taut rear. "Paige Glass." She bit her lip and looked down, scrunching her shoulders up. She slowly brought her eyes back to Paige's dancing green ones. "I was wondering, er, hoping, I mean, would you, um ... " she tried to get the next words out in a blur. "Would you go out with me sometime, like tonight?"

Paige laughed.

Eyes wide, Tamsin's mouth dropped open. "Are you laughing at me?"

Paige bit her lips closed, trying to stop her mirth, but her body continued to tremble. She shook her head, then took a breath and nodded. "I would love to." She rose on her tiptoes and gently kissed Tamsin. "You dork!"

They finished up breakfast and headed out the door. On the sidewalk between the two houses, Vernon stood with shoulders squared. His eyes practically glowed as he glared at them. "So, it's true; the two of you are shacking up together. Is that why you stole my new wolf?"

Paige's gaze snapped to Tamsin. "What is he talking about?"

"We've somehow formed a two-person pack. It happened pretty early on, shortly after you met the others. I didn't think it really mattered. At first, I planned on getting it sorted out before I left, but now, it really doesn't matter."

"Why doesn't it matter?" Vernon's voice was low. "Are you planning on killing me like you did Steve? You know I almost beat you. The all-powerful Tamsin who everyone has gushed on about all these years. You weren't so tough."

"Yep, not tough at all. But no; Paige's coming back to Chicago with me." Tamsin didn't care what Vernon thought about her.

"You are *not* taking away another one of my wolves, Tamsin Hath. She is mine."

"She hasn't been yours since the start. You never talked with her before changing her, and then you and Steve botched up everything. You should've brought her to Georgette and Orin right away, but no; you thought to keep her tucked away for some demented reason." Tamsin spoke low, but her anger threatened to spill over.

Vernon took a step towards them. "Do you think you could manage the pack any better? You, who've run from wolves for years?"

Tamsin felt the slap but brushed it off. "Yes, I do. But I think just about anyone could. What you've done with my family's legacy is a travesty. The Pacific Pack was one of the strongest in the country, old and well established, and in under a year you've gutted it."

Climbing the steps to get in her face, Vernon sneered. "I challenge you, Tamsin Hath, I challenge you for the leadership of the Pacific Pack."

"I was leaving town, Vernon. Why do this to yourself?"

"Because I want you dead for what you did to Steve."

"I won't have two broken ribs and other broken bones, you dolt. You can't beat me."

Vernon's face morphed into a mask of disgust. "You're nothing. I could take you in my sleep. An English teacher? I'm a firefighter who works out regularly. You may be taller, and arrogant as shit, but I'll bring you down ... six feet down." He spun on his heel. "I'll see you in the yard in an hour."

Tamsin rubbed her forehead. A headache began thrumming.

Paige wrapped her arms around her arm. "We could run. Go to Chicago right now. You don't have to do this. If he wins ... what happens to me? Can I survive without you? Do I want to? I've been studying this, and I get it. I'm convinced, even if they weren't romantic, Vernon and Steve connected at fourteen. Like we did a week ago."

Tamsin's fingers curled into fists. "I'm not going to lose. Vernon is trying to make his way back to Steve in the only way he knows how. He doesn't get it, but we do." She turned to Paige, her eyes soft. "I think you're right."

Paige touched her cheek. "I saw how haunted you were after your battle with Steve. It won't be easier this time."

"I know."

CHAPTER 34 - THE BATTLE ROYALE

Paige couldn't believe she stood in the backyard again. She watched the two wolves as they circled each other, trembling. *If Tamsin loses, I might as well die.*

Maria slid her hand in her. "Don't worry, Tamsin is the strongest wolf I know."

Paige's mouth felt like a desert. She nodded, her eyes never leaving the two wolves. "Do you do anything else back here, besides watch death matches?"

She gave her hand a squeeze. "Yes. Despite how it looks, more often than not, this is a lovely place to be. I hope one day you'll come to learn that."

Vernon attacked, his gray muzzle coming in low, snapping at Tamsin's front leg ... which wasn't there.

Tamsin flowed to the side and chomped at the back of Vernon's neck, tearing off a chunk of bloody fur.

The two backed away from each other, Vernon crouching down. Tamsin darted in low, slammed into the smaller wolf, and knocked him over.

Vernon clamped down on Tamsin's front leg, but Tamsin twisted, allowing her leg to crack in the move. Her teeth found Vernon's neck. The larger wolf jerked her head, and the small gray's head wrenched at an odd angle. A quick, brutal death.

Around Paige she heard the other pack members sighs.

"Thank the gods," Maria mumbled next to her.

Georgette snorted. "You expected any different? You knew Tamsin was the better, stronger wolf. We've talked about it to and from work."

"Knowing and experiencing it are two different things." Orin's deep voice of reason got everyone moving.

After a moment, Vernon's jaw relaxed, but one of his teeth was stuck in Tamsin's leg. She whined. Orin ran out to disentangle the two.

Paige approached slowly, then knelt in the grass. "Am I okay near you in this form? Are you okay, sexy lady?"

Tamsin flopped down in front of Paige. She rubbed her muzzle in the grass to remove any blood before laying her head across Paige's thighs. Her dark brown eyes, the same in this form, gazed up at her, sad and hopeful. Paige lifted her hand, fisted. She slowly extended it and relaxed her fingers. For the first time, she placed her hand on a werewolf, raking her fingers over Tamsin's head. The wolf's eyes fluttered closed.

After a few minutes, Tamsin backed up and began the shift. When she finished, she appeared in front of Paige on her hands and knees, head down, breathing hard. "I'm so sorry. This is not the date I promised you."

Paige lunged forward and wrapped her arms around the woman's neck. "As long as I have you, I don't care where we are. Haven't you figured this out yet?" Tamsin tensed, and Paige remembered the broken arm. "Oh crap. I'm hurting you!" She started to pull back, but Tamsin caught her.

"Don't you dare let go. I need you, now, and forever."

Orin's voice floated from behind her. "You know, the full moon is coming in the next few days.

You could probably pull out Paige's wolf. Let her build a good memory back here. Connie and I could deal with that."

Tamsin groaned. "I need a towel or robe. Food first, I can't shift again without it. She isn't going furry alone."

Once she'd eaten, the others gave Paige some privacy. Apparently, the others were okay hanging out naked during the shift, but Paige wasn't quite that bold. Tamsin asked Paige to get on her hands and knees in the backyard.

"Okay Paige, close your eyes, reach down; find that wild, new, furry friend within you. Relax into that wild side, then push it out."

Paige opened one of her eyes. "Relax *and* push? Does that even make sense?"

Tamsin kissed her forehead. She released her power and Paige shivered. "Come out, my friend."

A feeling like nothing she'd ever imagined came over her. Her muscles tensed.

"Relax. It's hard, but focus on relaxing, it'll make it easier." Tamsin's voice washed through her.

She tried, but the feelings of her body shifting, muscles cramping and moving, bones ... oh, God, she didn't want to think about what she felt and heard. Her face stretched and she kept her eyes closed. She didn't want to see anything that was happening as everything in her body jerked, stretched, shrank, and God, it hurt!

It took an eternity, yet, after only a moment, she wasn't on hands and knees anymore. She wiggled her fingers and toes, but that wasn't right. It felt different. She opened her eyes and looked down ... she had paws, and claws that dug into the dirt and grass. Looking up, she saw Tamsin, and her smile was everything.

"You are beautiful. I should've known a lady as pretty as you would be a sexy wolf. You're white as snow with a black snout," she tracked a finger down Paige's nose as she listed the off-colored areas. "Black ears, black paws, and a black tail. Beautiful. Give me a minute, and then we can play."

Once Tamsin wolfed out, the two ran and tumbled around the backyard. Connie and Orin came out to watch. After a few minutes, they asked if they could join in. Tamsin gazed at Paige who trotted over to them and wagged her tail. She wasn't sure what proper communication was as a wolf, but figured a happy tail would work.

The four played and Paige felt more and more comfortable with them as wolves, as odd as that sounded even to herself.

CHAPTER 35 - A NEW SHERIFF IN TOWN

Tamsin woke up before Paige. She watched the other woman sleep and marveled that she had a partner in life so well suited to her. She gently stroked her hand over Paige's cheek. Their date had been everything she'd hoped. A fancy dinner, a hotel with a jacuzzi tub, and the two of them acting like love-struck dorks. In other words, perfect.

Paige's eyes fluttered open. She smiled at

Tamsin. "Hey, sexy. Whatcha doing?"

"Trying to figure out why you'd link yourself to a lunk like me. You know, you're a very attractive wolf."

Paige curled into her. "I'm beginning to wonder, myself. My life has become insane since you've entered it. I had a pretty good thing going before you showed up."

"Oh, really?"

"Absolutely. Though, you could probably convince me I'm wrong with coffee and some food. Your cooking does things to me." She shut her eyes. "I probably shouldn't have admitted that. You're using my mostly-asleep brain against me."

With a smile, Tamsin leaned down to kiss her. "I like that you think I hadn't figured that out yet. Every time I cook, you make these lovely noises. It's seductive as hell. If we move into the pack house, we'll have to figure out a way to keep the others out; it would be less fun with an audience."

"Move ... what?" Paige's eyes widened.

"Maybe we can remodel and have a personal kitchen in our suite. Make our area more apartment-esque"

"What are you talking about? I haven't had coffee; I can't follow without caffeine."

Tamsin kissed her again. "You're so damn cute, and beautiful, and lovely, and seductive, and–"

Paige giggled. "Stop!"

Tamsin's hand played down Paige's face, resting it on her shoulder. "If I remember the area correctly, a kitchen could be added. I want to update the bathroom anyway, something similar to what Aunt Elinore had at her place. The pack can get the construction done while I finish out the school year. That way, when I relocate–"

"Tamsin, what the hell!"

She scooted back down, molding her body to Paige's. Tamsin groaned and caught her partner's mouth in a deep kiss, savoring her. She had to stop herself before she gave in to her every want. They'd done plenty of that the night before.

Breathing hard, she rested her forehead against Paige's. "The pack can't go on without an alpha. I could call around, see if any pack has a wolf strong enough, or, I can take my place in the pack my family has run since it was established by my great-grandparents. The others weren't wrong. The Pacific Pack is my legacy. It's why I left when I did; Uncle Clyde wanted a chance to run it, and I couldn't be in a pack with any alpha but my dad."

Paige nodded. "Why didn't you return after he died?"

"I don't know. I'd gotten it in my head I was a lone wolf and didn't need anyone else. Everyone told me I was insane; I should find someone to connect with. I resisted and was hurting inside. I ignored it all, until you came along and pushed past all my built-up walls."

"Good, you needed someone to bully you around. I'm glad that someone could be me. But are you saying, in all those years, there wasn't anyone else?"

Tamsin laughed. "You're asking about competition? Well, I'd closed myself off. If I hadn't, there may have been someone in Chicago, I don't know. The pack there kept asking me to join. Actually, I don't know if that's true; one member of the pack kept asking me to join. He was my only contact with the pack. That sometimes happens. A lone wolf has one person they communicate with. For me, it was Nolan."

"Did you ever want to ... I don't know, connect with Nolan?"

"What is this? Trying to get rid of me already?"

"No, just trying to figure out why I was the one who broke through."

"Because, Ms. Glass, you are the one who saw me, and touched my heart."

By the afternoon they'd made it back to Santa

Cruz. They drove directly to the pack house and found the others all there.

"You're back!" Maria leapt up to hug them both. "I wasn't sure if we'd see you again before you went back to Chicago."

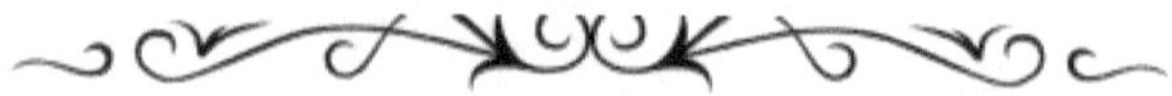

"Tamsin, your great-grandparents started this pack. It's your legacy. My one hope is that one day, you will take it over, and then your kids, and so on. We are a strong and proud line, and the pack is powerful because of it."

Tamsin gazed up into her dad's eyes with pride, hoping she could live up to the tradition of her family.

Tamsin held Paige's hand and led her to a love seat on the far side of the living room. "I can't leave you without an alpha; I know that. This pack is my family's legacy, as you all keep reminding me. I also can't leave my responsibilities back in Chicago."

Connie squealed. "You're coming back in June, aren't you?"

She smiled. "I am. Once the school year is over,

I'll come back. Over the next few months, I'll close up any loose ends I have in Chicago so I can move my life back here. Spring break just ended, so I'll be back in under two months."

Orin's brows came together. "I know you've lived alone a long time, but you've been with Paige for the last few weeks. Will you be able to go back to solitude for that long?"

"I'm going to go with her," Paige said. "She won't be alone. I'm not sure either of us would be comfortable separated for two months. I don't understand everything that happened when Steve bit me. This werewolf gig is still crazy to me, but I've learned that much."

The others relaxed. They discussed plans for the house and the pack for the next few months. Paige would fly to Chicago after Tamsin; someone had put an offer on her house, and she needed to stay to sign papers.

CHAPTER 36 – A NEW FAMILY

Paige gazed at these new strangers that were becoming more and more a family, something she'd never had before. "Can we ..." She stopped. She wasn't sure how to ask.

"What do you want?" Tamsin asked next to her, her hand sliding onto her knee.

"Nothing, it's silly." Paige bit her lip. This whole new world was so new. She had no idea what the rules were. She just knew the day before, when she'd become a wolf for the first time. *I can't believe I just thought that ... me, a werewolf! But it was so much fun.*

Connie laughed. "All you natural born wolves, you have no idea!" She looked at Paige. "You want to shift again, don't you."

It didn't take long for everyone to agree. Paige got on her hands and knees. Sinking deep into a new part of her belly, she found a furry, untamed part of herself and invited it out. A wash of pain flowed over her, fast and wild, and then the world changed. Colors dimmed, scents intensified, and she wanted to run!

FIND THE NEXT BOOK

Wolf Magic, here

https://www.amazon.com/dp/B0BZV3ZVP7

WHERE TO FIND HARLOWE FROST

Thanks for reading!

Find more of my books on my website:

http://hannahwillowauthor.com

You can also find me on:

Twitter: @hannahwillow217

Instagram: @hannahwillow217

Facebook Hannah Willow

Harlowe Frost has been a teacher at both the high school and college level. Her parents instilled a love of reading from a young age. She grew up in the queer community. Her favorite genre growing up was fantasy and science fiction, that is, until she discovered urban fantasy and paranormal romance. What she never found in those books was the diversity in background, gender identity, and sexuality she saw in the people around her. She decided if she couldn't find that in what she read, then she would write it herself. This started her writing paranormal romance with a LGBTQ+ background.